"Would you Dr. Douglas?"

"He's a scientist who works at the university. I'm supposed to meet him here, but I don't know what he looks like. I assume he's an older guy, probably with glasses." Katie glanced around, searching for the man, hoping maybe she'd catch his eye and he'd introduce himself.

A man turned to face Katie. The only thing she saw was the devastating smile, and his azure eyes. For a moment she couldn't breathe. Her heart stopped and heat spread through her lower extremities.

He's freakin' gorgeous.

"He was around earlier this evening, but I think he may have left." The man smiled at her again then glanced around the pub. "I don't see him. Why did you need him?"

Holy hell on a biscuit. If he smiles one more time like that I might have to jump him right here in the middle of the bar.

Katie was no prude, but it had been a long time since her body responded like this to a man, especially one she didn't know.

If he can do that with a look, imagine what it would be like if he touched me...

Dear Reader,

Have you ever been burned by love so badly that you thought you'd never have another relationship? Most of us have at some point in our lives and that's what I wanted to explore in *She Who Dares, Wins*. We have Katie McClure, a private detective who hasn't had a lot of luck in love. She finds herself falling hard for her client, Professor Macon Douglas, who is a deadly combination of smart, funny and incredibly hot. It's her job to find out who's behind the mysterious incidents that have put Mac's life in danger.

Mac wants Katie, the sexiest bodyguard he's ever seen, and he doesn't care what he has to do to get her. His refusal to take the threats against him seriously drives Katie crazy. Can she save his life before it's too late? Can he convince Katie that he's worth putting all of her past troubles behind her? You'll have to wait and see if she takes him up on his dare to love again.

Please email me at candacehavensbook@gmail.com and tell me what you think about the book. You can also find me on twitter.com/candacehavens and MySpace, Facebook and Live Journal. I look forward to hearing from you.

Enjoy!

Candace Havens

Candace Havens

SHE WHO DARES, WINS

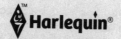

TORONTO NEW YORK LONDON
AMSTERDAM PARIS SYDNEY HAMBURG
STOCKHOLM ATHENS TOKYO MILAN MADRID
PRAGUE WARSAW BUDAPEST AUCKLAND

Recycling programs
for this product may
not exist in your area.

ISBN-13: 978-0-373-79611-3

SHE WHO DARES, WINS

ABOUT THE AUTHOR

Award-winning author and columnist Candace "Candy" Havens lives in Texas with her mostly understanding husband, two children and two dogs, Scoobie and Gizmo. Candy is a nationally syndicated entertainment columnist for FYI Television. She has interviewed just about everyone in Hollywood from George Clooney and Orlando Bloom to Nicole Kidman and Kate Beckinsale. You can hear Candy weekly on The Big 96.3 in the Dallas–Fort Worth Area. Her popular online writer's workshop has more than thirteen hundred students and provides free classes to professional and aspiring writers.

Books by Candace Havens

HARLEQUIN BLAZE
523—TAKE ME IF YOU DARE

To get the inside scoop on Harlequin Blaze and its talented writers, be sure to check out blazeauthors.com.

Don't miss any of our special offers. Write to us at the following address for information on our newest releases.

Harlequin Reader Service
U.S.: 3010 Walden Ave., P.O. Box 1325, Buffalo, NY 14269
Canadian: P.O. Box 609, Fort Erie, Ont. L2A 5X3

I'd like to dedicate this book to
Shannon Canard and Rosemary Clement Moore,
who are the best friends a girl ever had
and share my love for the world of romance.

Prologue

MACON BLINKED several times as the road blurred before him. "I shouldn't have had a pint at the pub," he whispered as he rubbed the bridge of his nose. But one lager didn't explain the tiredness blanketing him, making it difficult to keep his eyes open.

The dark, curvy road was barely large enough for one car to pass, and for the third time in an hour he wondered about his sanity choosing to drive from London to the country so late at night to visit a greenhouse. The incessant rain didn't help a damn thing. Macon reached to adjust his glasses but only managed to knock them off his nose.

Oh, hell.

Checking the rearview, he made sure no one was behind him before he reached down to grab the glasses.

Slamming them on his face, he glanced back at the road in time to see lights from an oncoming vehicle flash before him. He had no choice but to swerve.

His car raced over the embankment and into the trees, screeching tires and air bag powder in his eyes the last things he remembered.

1

KATIE'S STOMACH FLUTTERED with nervous energy as her fist tightened around her cell phone. This happened when she opened a new case. The excitement was heightened by her first transatlantic job for the agency, and the fact that she had no idea what lay ahead. The London taxi zipped away from the curb at Heathrow and into traffic. If she hadn't been holding the handle she would have been tossed to the other side of the seat.

Eventually they reached the city center and the driver called out, "Piccadilly Square" in an accent so heavy she could barely understand him. She nodded and stared down at her phone. Her boss and best friend at Stonegate Investigative Agency, Mariska, had emailed several files about their new client.

Unfortunately just as she'd been about to download case notes, Katie's phone had died midflight and she hadn't been able to recharge it thanks to checking the charger in with her bags. She had no idea what the man looked like, or any other information except where she was supposed to meet him.

And I'm already a half hour late.

The professor had been involved in an incident, which was why Katie was in London. Dr. Douglas, an environmental scientist, claimed he'd been run off the road and into a tree. Paint scrapes on his car were the only proof. While there had been alcohol in his system, it had been minimal. The police were tracking the paint, but they didn't have the whole story. The dean at the university where the professor worked wanted to keep the matter quiet, so the accident was being treated as a one-time event.

That wasn't the truth. It was the second time something life-threatening had happened to the professor in the past two weeks.

There had also been some odd phone calls to the dean intimating Douglas should stop his research, and the professor had been mugged the night before the last accident. The dean worried that they were dealing with a radical or worse, a terrorist group, but he didn't want to involve the police unless absolutely necessary.

"That's the high court." The driver interrupted her thoughts. "Fancy place for fancy folk. There is the museum." The cabbie continued his tour-guide duties and Katie wondered if it would be rude to pay him to stop talking.

Stop it. It's not his fault you're having a crappy day.

She glanced out the window so it at least looked as if she were interested, and tried to gather her thoughts.

It seemed from what information Katie had that the dean was concerned about protecting the university's reputation, rather than the safety of Dr. Douglas. Katie felt a little sorry for the old man.

The professor's research was classified by the British

government, which meant Stonegate couldn't come up with much in that regard. Even the dean had refused to discuss it on the phone, telling them Katie would need special clearance once she arrived in London.

Whatever the project might be didn't really matter. Katie's job was to determine if there was a real threat, eliminate it and look after the dotty professor. This whole thing was a personal favor to the dean, who had been a dear friend of the mother of Katie's boss and best friend, Mariska.

If Katie had had her way, she would have avoided the trip and sent the case straight to Scotland Yard where it belonged, but the decision wasn't hers.

The taxi stopped on a brick-lined street in front of a pub straight out of a Dickens tale. Katie glanced at the meter and was shocked to see how much it was. Didn't matter where in the world you were, cabs were expensive. She tossed some pound notes to the driver and stepped out with her small rolling suitcase and laptop bag.

The Seven Stars, the pub where she was to meet the professor, looked exactly like what she thought an English pub would from the outside—dark wood with brass. It had an old-world feel. Rolling her case through the door, with her laptop bag on her shoulder, she stood there for a moment allowing her eyes to adjust. The smell of beer and food was comforting in a way, and she let herself relax for a few seconds while she surveyed the room.

She was a detective—she should be able to spot one dotty old professor.

It was seven-thirty and the place was crowded with people. She had wanted to meet the professor and the dean at the university, but Dr. Douglas had insisted on the pub. The place did have a familiarity about it, reminding her of her mom and dad's bar back in the Bronx.

The only things missing were her were nosy, boisterous brothers and her adorable Grandpa Joe behind the bar telling his stories about walking the beat years ago. He was the family member she missed most. GJ, as she called him, was the only sane one in the bunch, and he insisted Katie follow her dreams no matter where they led her.

GJ, a former cop, had been the one to help her get into the academy back in the Bronx. He'd pushed her to be a detective, even when everyone else in her family thought it was a ludicrous idea. They believed she should settle down and have babies with Jay Spiloli.

Ugh. Remembering Jay made her gut churn with nastiness. She'd dated him for a couple of weeks, only to learn he'd been cheating on her the whole time with Missy Ringovitz. The night she found out, she made her brothers lock her in her room so she couldn't kill Jay. Her only satisfaction came the next day when she saw his face had taken a beating, probably due to her brothers' fists. Though they would never tell her the truth about it.

It didn't matter. Having babies with Jay was so not in the cards for her. She'd followed her grandpa's advice, and three years as a detective had prepared her for this job of a lifetime working at Stonegate, where she traveled the world solving cases.

She glanced around the room, but didn't see any dotty-looking prof types. Most of the people there were in their mid-thirties and wore three-piece suits. Even the women had donned heels with suits. A bunch of Wall Street types, only she was on the wrong continent.

Bartenders tend to know everything going on in their establishments. I might as well start there.

Katie headed for the intricately carved bar, which wasn't easy in the crowd with her laptop and suitcase in tow.

"Hey, would you happen to know a Dr. Douglas?" Katie maneuvered her suitcase between the bar stools. The bartender delivered a pint to the man next to her and looked up.

"I know a few, lass. It's a common name 'round here."

Well, hell.

"He's a scientist and works at the university. I'm supposed to meet him here, but I don't know what he looks like. I assume he's an older guy, probably with glasses." She glanced around searching for the man, hoping maybe she'd catch his eye and he'd introduce himself.

The bartender nodded. "Ah, I see." He moved in front of the man with the pint. "Don't suppose you've seen the doc?"

The man turned to face Katie. The only thing she saw for a few seconds was the devastating smile and his azure eyes. She couldn't breathe. Her heart stopped and heat spread through her lower extremities.

He's freakin' gorgeous.

"He was around earlier this evening, but I think he may have left." The hunk of hotness smiled at her again, then glanced around the pub. "I don't see him. Why did you need him?"

Holy hell on a biscuit. If he smiles like that again

I might have to jump him right here in the middle of the bar.

Katie was no prude, but it had been a long time since her body had responded like that to a man, especially one she didn't know.

If he can do that with a look, imagine what it would be like if he touched me.

Her body quivered with the very thought of it.

When his right eyebrow rose, she realized she was supposed to say something. His words finally penetrated her sex-addled brain. "Wh-what? Oh—I..." she stammered. "I was only—" she checked her watch "—a half hour late. It took me forever to get through customs. So you know the professor?"

The hottie leaned an elbow against the bar. "I know of him."

Katie chewed on her lip. "Hmm. Well, I guess I'll have to find him at the university."

"I wouldn't bother. I'm sure he's headed home to bed. It is almost eight," he said as he looked at his watch.

The bartender grunted at that.

Katie deflated as she sat down on the stool next to the man. "I'm not surprised. It's been that kind of day for me." She'd almost missed her flight because of car trouble, her phone wasn't working right and she'd missed the meeting with the professor.

"Sounds to me like you could use one of these." The bartender set a pint in front of her.

"He's right, you know." The handsome man waved a hand toward the beer. "Nothing like a good pint to set the world right again."

Katie worried about the professor's safety, but she didn't have any private contact info for him or the dean.

All she had were the numbers for the university. Hopefully the old man had made it home safely.

She might as well have a drink and then head to the hotel so she could start fresh in the morning. She was already feeling the jet lag Mariska had warned her about. Her boss had insisted Katie try to sleep on the plane, but she could never get comfortable. A beer would help her relax and then she could get a good night's rest.

"What the heck." She held up her glass. "Cheers."

THE SMOKY VOICE and New York accent were at odds with the petite brunette at Macon's side. He had a difficult time believing this woman was Katie McClure, the bodyguard sent to protect him. He was an ass for not confessing his identity, but he wanted to have a little fun. If she were as good at her job as the dean said, she'd figure it out eventually.

"I must be tired." She laughed. "I just realized you're American. I'd say somewhere on the West Coast."

He liked the deep throaty laugh, and she had the most beautiful chocolate eyes framed by long lashes. There was something in those eyes, a slight hardness, that told him she'd seen more than most people, but she looked far too young for that.

"You're right. That's quite an ear you have," he said.

"I don't know about that. I'm having the toughest time understanding people here, which makes me feel like an idiot, since we speak the same language."

Macon laughed. "You get used to it eventually. I'm a surfer boy from Laguna, and I even picked up a few of the phrases. Caught myself saying 'bloody hell' the other day. And like America there are different types of accents. Some are easier to understand than others."

"The Bronx where I grew up is a melting pot of accents and you never know what you might get when you say hello to someone."

He liked this woman. Beyond the fact that she was gorgeous, her no-nonsense attitude and directness were refreshing.

"Well, fellow American. Don't suppose you'd let me buy you dinner?" Macon surprised himself with the question. The words had burst out of his mouth before he could stop them. He couldn't remember the last time he'd asked a woman out.

Her eyes flashed with surprise, and he expected a quick no.

She gave him the once-over. "I could eat." She sniffed the air. "And if the food is half as good as it smells, I'm in."

"Timothy, looks like we'll need some menus. And perhaps a table," Macon told the bartender.

Mac had rolled up his sleeves earlier in the evening, and when Katie put a hand on his arm, the skin-to-skin contact sent his libido into overdrive.

"Nah, I'm good sitting here at the bar." She gave him a quick smile. "Done it most of my life."

"Oh, really. I didn't take you for the AA type."

"You're a funny one." She smirked. "GJ, my grandpa, and my parents own a pub in the Bronx populated by their friends who are all cops. So I spent a lot of time there doing my homework at the bar or at one of the tables in the back."

That explained why she'd gone into law enforcement. She still didn't fit the big Amazon image he had in his head of the security agent sent to protect him. She was more ballerina than bodyguard.

Timothy handed them each a menu. Macon didn't need to look at it, as he'd been eating there most nights for the past four years. It was close to his apartment and he was a big fan of the food.

She slipped off her jacket and he glimpsed her nearly perfect figure—a petite goddess in one amazing package. His body tightened with need and he had to think of nice cold showers in order to avoid her seeing just how happy he was to meet her.

He watched as she perused the menu. "If you like a good steak, they know how to do it right and the Caesar salad is one of my favorites," he offered.

"That'll work for me." She handed the menu back to the bartender as he took their order.

"This place was pretty crowded earlier. Where did everyone go?" She twirled around on the bar stool, their knees rubbing together for a second, and again his body reacted. What was it about her? The scientist in him wondered about pheromones, but he forced himself to push those thoughts aside so he could answer her questions.

"Most of them work at the high court—barristers and clerks, and maybe a few judges. Everybody will have gone home to their families. In about an hour there will be an influx of partiers out for a good time. The crowd changes and it gets louder as the night goes on."

She shook her head. "It really does feel like home—almost makes me miss it."

"Almost?" From the way she said it, he could tell she had mixed feelings.

"Like most people, I have some family baggage." She

blew out a breath. "I'm Katie, by the way." She stuck out a hand for him to shake.

"I'm M—" He'd almost said Macon. "Mac, that's what my friends call me."

The bartender grunted again as he put their salads on the bar.

"Wow! Now, that's a salad." She laughed at the sight of the large bowl filled to the brim with vegetables. The sound of her laugh was like a warm blanket wrapped around him—a warm sexy blanket.

He cleared his throat. "Roxy, the chef here, likes to make sure her customers are well fed."

As they chatted through dinner he noticed she ate every bite of her meal, and she downed two more pints. But she was as clear-eyed as when she'd walked in.

Mac on the other hand was feeling the effects of the beer. He was far from drunk, but he was more relaxed than he'd been in months.

When they finished their meals, she opened her bag to pull out some pound notes.

"Hey, I'm buying you dinner, remember?" He handed the bills she'd put on the bar back to her.

Katie shook her head. "Nah. If you'd been a boring ass, I'd make you pay. But I had fun talking to you. We'll go Dutch."

Macon and the bartender both guffawed. "It's difficult to argue with logic like that," he said, "but I, as a gentleman, would feel less of a man if you paid."

Katie rolled her eyes. "Men. You're the same everywhere I go. Fine. Pay." She held out her hand. "Thank you for a lovely meal."

He took her hand in his. "I had more fun tonight than I've had in months. I can't remember the last time I had a—" He'd been about to say date, which wasn't the right word. "A good meal with a beautiful woman."

She blushed. Now, that was unexpected.

"I wish you'd let me walk you to your next destination. It can be tough to get a taxi this time of night, and some of the streets can be a bit dodgy."

She put her hands on her hips. "Mac, are you hitting on me?"

God, she was forthright. "Yes," he answered honestly.

She laughed out loud. "What if you're some kind of ax murderer and you're only saying pretty things to get me alone?"

"Oh, I want you alone, but there are no axes in the picture. Besides, Timothy will vouch for me. Right?"

Timothy grunted and rolled his eyes. "He's better than most."

"Now, that's a rousing referral if ever I heard one." Katie smiled.

Macon knew he should tell her who he was, but he had a feeling if he did, this connection with her would be broken. He wanted her, and if it meant withholding information for the greater good, who was he to complain? It had been so long since he'd felt any kind of connection with anyone. For the past six years everything had been about his work. He deserved some fun.

Okay, he was an ass. But he wanted this woman, and the feeling persisted that if she knew the truth all bets would be off.

He grabbed her bag with one hand and held her hand with the other.

"So where are we off to next?" he said as they stepped out onto the sidewalk.

"To the Dorchester," she replied breathlessly, another blush creeping up on her cheeks, but not connected with the London chill.

She's so tough, but blushes. This woman intrigued him and he had to know more about her.

Macon had several blocks to convince her why spending the night with him would be the best thing that ever happened to her. And then he would tell her the truth.

2

KATIE STOOD BESIDE MAC on the elevator chewing her lip.

What am I doing?

When Mac had offered to take Katie's bags upstairs to her suite at the Dorchester, she'd known what he meant, and she wanted it. She wanted him. Knowing him for less than two hours didn't matter. They had a connection unlike any she'd ever experienced.

When she left New York, she'd been determined to change her life. She would no longer be consumed by work and she'd start dating again. It hadn't happened that way. The move to Texas to help Mariska settle in at the agency had left Katie with less free time than ever. Not that she minded at first. It had been exciting picking up the pieces and helping her friend keep the agency running.

Stonegate Investigative Agency was stronger than ever, and Katie didn't have to carry the success of the business on her shoulders. Well, she'd never been alone—her friends Chi and Makala had been there, too—but Katie had been responsible for the day-to-day operations.

The only time she'd kissed a guy in the past six months had been on a case when she'd gone undercover with a DEA agent. Sad, that was the only way she could get a man to touch her, but it was the truth. She was like some kind of social pariah when it came to the opposite sex.

Her mother had always said she was too tough, but Katie couldn't help it. That was her nature, and if a guy couldn't handle it, well, to hell with him.

But Mac was different. He saw her as a woman. He didn't have any preconceived notions about her past and he didn't seem to care about anything except the now.

The elevator dinged and the doors slid open.

Could she do this? Could she have a one-night stand in a foreign country with a man she barely knew?

His hand touched her back to lead her off the elevator and a shiver of delight warmed her.

Yes. She most definitely could spend a night with this stranger.

Everything about him, from his tall, lanky surfer-boy looks to his deep melodic voice, screamed hot juicy sex. Didn't she deserve one night with this man she knew instinctively could do dangerous and wonderful things to her?

They arrived at the door much too quickly. She slipped the key card in and the handle turned.

"Well, here we are." He handed her the bag. "Thank you for a great night. I'm more relaxed than I've been in months. I don't run into many Americans in my social circles, and it's been nice talking about home with you." He dazzled her with that smile again.

Wait. This was good-night? Katie was so confused. Had she read the signals wrong?

Then she saw it in his eyes—that moment where he was giving her an out. He didn't want to pressure her into anything, and it made her want him even more.

"We never had dessert," she said, her voice husky with need. She opened the door and pushed the case inside, holding the door for him to step through.

He watched her, as if he were trying to get a read.

She gave him a quick grin, and that was all it took.

Stepping in, he shut the door.

"Are you really hungry?" Mac asked as he brushed a hair away from her cheek. That brief touch sent shudders through her body.

Katie leaned back against the wall just inside the suite. The desire in his eyes made her belly tighten, and she didn't trust her voice, so she shook her head.

He leaned in and kissed her, teasing at first with light touches to her lips. Katie restrained herself from shoving him to the floor and taking him right then and there, as his kisses caused a tingling straight through her from where their lips met.

Mac was so much taller and she found herself rising to the tips of her toes so she could taste more of him. All the tiredness and worry slipped from her mind as his hands slid around her waist, pulling her toward him.

They tasted each other for a good five minutes. With their tongues dancing and exploring, she couldn't get enough of his steak-and-dark-beer-mixed-with-peppermint flavor.

She wound her arms around his neck. His erection pressed into her belly, giving her such a sense of power she nearly growled. Mac didn't know it, but he'd become her prey. She wanted him now, inside her.

"Too many clothes," she whispered against his lips. Pulling her arms away, she unbuttoned his shirt. When her nervous fingers fumbled, it took great restraint to keep from ripping the material so she could feel his skin.

He lifted his lips from hers and smiled. Gently shoving her hands away from his shirt, he reached for hers, sliding it off her shoulders and exposing her pink bra. He made quick work of her pants, which were wide legged and slipped to the floor.

Katie refused to let him have all the fun. She unzipped his jeans, the feel of him hard and tight against her palm as she groped him.

He moaned and moved her so he was against the wall to brace them. She stopped stroking him long enough to pull her boots off, but he stopped her.

"Leave them on," he said heavily as he tugged the panties past them.

He knelt, leaving a trail of kisses on her neck, breasts and stomach. When his tongue reached its destination, Katie threw her head back, balancing her hands on his shoulders as he laved her hot pink flesh with such precision that in mere seconds her body quaked with a mind-blowing orgasm.

Before Katie could pass out from the sheer pleasure of it, he scooped her up in his arms and tossed her gently onto the bed. Once again he knelt, teasing her until she writhed before him. Her boots wrapped around his shoulders as he continued to drive her to the brink, this time the orgasm so intense she saw tiny specks of light behind her eyes.

"I could watch you do that all night." Mac's voice was deeper than before. "And these boots—you're so damn gorgeous."

Katie couldn't hide her smile. His words made her feel empowered.

She reached for him. "I need you inside me, please, Mac. Please," she begged. She could no longer wait for his cock to give her the relief she needed.

"Not yet, love," he said as he slid up her body, bringing both her breasts to hard peaks with his mouth as his fingers pumped in and out of her pink flesh. She wasn't sure how much more she could take.

Her fingers grabbed his hair. "Now. I need you now."

That seemed to do it.

He yanked his shirt over his head and released his cock from his pants. He fumbled with something in his pocket and she realized he was grabbing a condom. At least he'd thought of it—she hadn't.

She sat up, took the package from his hand and ripped it open, sheathing him with the protection as fast as possible. He was long, hard and thick. She lifted her legs, still clad in the boots, up over his shoulders as she guided him into her.

When there was a long pause she worried for a second that maybe he was too big, but he pumped her gently a few times, covering his cock in her juices, and her body opened to him. The pace quickened and soon he was pounding her with such ferocity her body came unglued. When his finger touched her nub, she screamed her release.

The look of desire in his eyes as he watched her come sent waves of pleasure through her. Every muscle in her body tightened as he was bringing her to yet another orgasm.

"Come with me," she begged. "I want to watch you come with me."

The pounding increased and his thumb rubbed her nub again as Katie writhed on the bed, uncertain how much more her body could take, but she wanted him more than anything.

His blue eyes centered on her as he moaned, "Katie," and she felt such power in those words.

"Yes, Mac. Come with me. Ohhhhhh." She was lost then in the sensation of him, their bodies echoing the pleasure they both experienced. When he moaned her name again, his body stiffened with release just as her entire body quaked with an orgasm. This time she saw more tiny stars in her lids, and every muscle turned to rubber.

When he slid out, she moaned her complaint.

"Have to sit." His words came out on a pant. "You're amazing."

"No." She was still winded. "That was all you. I was along for the ride. One wonderful, wild ride."

He took care of the condom, then lay beside her sideways, their legs hanging off the edge. Normally Katie would have felt the need to cover herself, but the way he looked at her as if she were a big piece of chocolate he couldn't wait to devour made her comfortable in her own skin.

He put his arm behind her and pulled her closer to him. "Trust me when I tell you we were on that ride together."

She snuggled into him, but couldn't stifle a yawn.

"You're tired." He turned so he could see her face.

"Nah, that was a sign of contentment, nothing more."

"Hmm." He pulled away. "I think maybe we should get you ready for bed."

She sighed. "We are in bed."

He chuckled at that.

"True," he said as he sat up, and then he reached down and slid her boots off.

Another yawn escaped. Damn. She didn't want to fall asleep.

Mac picked her up with one arm so she was nestled against him. Using his other arm he pulled the covers back. "Let's at least get you warm."

Carefully he put her back down and moved her legs under the covers, intimate and sweet at the same time.

Something clicked for Katie. "Oh, wow. I'm probably keeping you from one of those quick exits guys like to make. Sorry, I don't do this—uh, well, I've never slept with a guy I don't really know." She grinned. Katie wondered why she couldn't shut up. Normally she wasn't the talkative type, but her nerves had returned.

Mac touched her cheek. "No, I can promise you I don't want to go right now." He held her tighter and nuzzled his nose at her neck.

Katie sighed with contentment. Mac spoke the truth for now. She was good at reading people. Maybe he wouldn't leave right away, but he would eventually. The idea made her a little sad.

"I have to say I'm kind of glad the professor wasn't there tonight."

A weird look passed over his face. "What do you mean?"

"I wouldn't have met you, and we'd have missed this crazy-good night together. Thank you."

He leaned down and kissed her. "It was definitely crazy good."

She yawned again. "I'm about to fall asleep." Her eyes were so heavy she could barely keep them open. "Damn you for being so good with the sex. You wore me out."

This time he laughed out loud. He sat next to her, brushing the hair away from her face. "You have to take some of that blame, you know. You're pretty damn good with the sex, too."

Katie smiled with satisfaction. No one had ever said she was good in bed. Not that she'd had many lovers.

"I like you," she said.

He kissed her again tenderly. "I like you, too."

YOU'RE AN ASS. Mac couldn't believe he'd failed to tell Katie the truth before she fell asleep. He'd made mad, passionate love with her, and then he'd lied to her.

Not so much a lie as an omission. He had a feeling she wouldn't see it that way. What he'd done was wrong, and he knew it. The opportunity to tell her had come about more than once during their evening together, but their evening had been so perfect, he didn't want it to end. This had been one of the best nights of his life, and not just the sex. Though that had been incredible. He'd enjoyed their chat during dinner. She was honest and forthright, and he was absolutely charmed by her.

Sitting there for a moment on her bed, he watched her sleep. She was nothing short of gorgeous. From her head down to those purple-painted toenails he'd seen when he slipped her boots and socks off her feet.

Those boots. He took a deep breath. Katie's lithe

body, naked with only those boots, was a memory burned into his brain for a lifetime.

That's good, since she's probably never going to speak to you again when she finds out the truth.

He'd figure something out. He had to, because after finding the woman of his dreams, he wasn't about to let her go. Katie was everything he hadn't known he wanted, and she was perfect. A combination of strength, femininity and sensuality, which stirred his baser instincts in a way no other woman had.

I need a strategy—a plan to keep Katie McClure in my life.

At least until he could see where this thing between them was going. She thought it a one-night stand, but he'd heard the disappointment in her voice. She still wanted him, and that was something perhaps he could use to his advantage.

His lab. He needed those familiar white and gray walls in order to think.

Macon left the Dorchester determined to find a way to make Katie forgive him.

3

FOR SOMEONE WHO THRIVED on punctuality, Katie had made a mess of her appointments the past twenty-four hours. After waking up at five in the morning, naked in her bed, it had taken her a few minutes to discern where she was. Mortified, she realized she'd fallen asleep while Mac was still there. By the time she'd opened her eyes he was long gone.

At first she was disappointed he hadn't left a note, but she quickly admonished herself. It was about the moment and having some fun—hadn't her friend Mar told her to do exactly that? Once this case was over, she'd been ordered to take some time off and relax. It had been years since Katie had had a vacation—she wasn't sure she remembered how.

In fact, she might stay at the Dorchester and enjoy the amenities. The two-bedroom suite Mar had insisted Katie stay in was bigger than her entire apartment in Texas, and it was the most luxurious place she'd ever slept in. There were two bedrooms in case she had to move the professor to a safer location. The bathtub alone was as big as a boat, and in the daylight she'd explored the cavernous suite to discover everything from state-of-the art electronics to a showerhead with so many different spouts it felt as if she was getting a massage.

She'd called the university at eight to set an appointment with the dean and the professor. The dean's assistant told her he wasn't in, but she did set a meeting with the professor. The appointment was for nine, and Katie was stuck in traffic that was worse than midtown Manhattan during rush hour.

Great. She couldn't call the school from the car because in her foggy state earlier in the morning, she'd accidentally plugged her phone and computer into the socket before she realized she'd used the wrong adapter. A zip and a pop later, both were fried.

Katie had congratulated herself for not tossing both of the electronics out the French doors of her suite. Using the hotel phone she'd called Mar and told her what had happened. Her friend had laughed.

"Even if you use the right adapter, half the time it'll fry your electronics. I should have warned you," Mar apologized.

"It's not your fault. I picked the package of adapters up at the airport, but I must have read the instructions wrong."

"No worries, Katie. We'll have new, fully loaded electronics to you by tomorrow."

Mar didn't know Katie's entire life was on her phone and computer. She felt naked without them. The upside was her busy family couldn't contact her. She'd find a way to phone or email her mom later and let her know she was safe. Otherwise, that would be all she heard for the next two months. No less than ten voice mails a day about what an ungrateful daughter she was.

Katie chuckled. More than once Mar had told her to appreciate how lucky she was to have a family who cared so much.

The McClures cared too much, as far as Katie was concerned.

While she waited in the cab she ran over the mental notes she'd made the day before. The professor's research had something to do with food sources for third world countries. For some reason, the government was involved and the project was under extreme security.

It was her job to determine if the threats were real and to protect him until they could figure out what was going on. She'd look after the dotty old man and see what she could find out. The physical evidence would be her first priority. There was so much more they could do now with the state-of-the-art labs at Stonegate.

"Almost there, miss, the building on the right," the cab driver said. In the heart of London she'd expected a bunch of historic buildings, since the college had been around a few hundred years. There were some of those across the street, but this science building was a modern expanse of glass and steel.

After paying the cab, she walked in. The redheaded security officer, with a name badge claiming he was George, checked her credentials carefully. Then he asked to see her bag, and he seemed to linger over the small pocket where she'd stored her makeup. Picking up her perfume, he sniffed and closed his eyes.

When he glanced up and saw her eyebrow up, he quickly put the perfume back and closed the bag.

"Good to go, then." He handed her an access card with his face flushed. "Use this in the lift to go to the third floor."

On the third floor she followed the numbers until she reached the steel door that read Lab 314. Using the card she entered.

"Please strip and step into the shower. Then walk through the back door, where you'll find a suit," a voice said through a speaker as soon as she entered a narrow hallway. It was all white with a shower and hooks on the wall. Katie rolled her eyes. "Is that really necessary? I'm here to see Professor Macon Douglas."

"Have you been traveling?" the voice said through the box.

"Yes."

"Then you'll have to wear a suit to talk to the professor. We can't risk spore contamination."

Great. Whatever.

She pulled off her black blazer and hopped on one foot and then the other so she could slip off her boots. The white T-shirt and dark jeans, her everyday uniform now, were next. If the pervy lab assistant watched her, he was about to get an eyeful as she lost the black thong and matching bra. Nudity wasn't something she was that modest about. She'd grown up in a house with brothers, where privacy was a luxury.

She stepped into the shower, surprised when a soft powdery mist coated her skin instead of water. The powder, which had a strange pine-and-earth scent, dissipated as soon as it touched her, but it left her feeling fresher than when she'd stepped in. After thirty seconds it shut off.

"I feel like I'm in some weird sci-fi movie," she whispered.

The metal door on the other side of the dry shower slid open and she made her way through into another room not much bigger than a walk-in closet. The suit the voice had mentioned was nothing more than sweats, none of which fit her five-foot-three, petite frame. She found the one labeled Small and tied the string as tight as she could around her waist. The sweatshirt swallowed her, and dark green was so not her color, but she pushed up the sleeves and made it work.

I should have demanded we meet in the dean's office. This is crazy.

Once she was dressed, another door clicked open and she pushed her way through into the lab, which was filled with computer equipment, strange machines and a giant dry erase board with all kinds of equations on it.

A man dressed in jeans had his back to her. He was tall and lanky and looked just like—

"What are you doing here?" Katie couldn't believe her eyes when he turned around.

"Hi," Mac said.

"You…work here?"

He nodded.

"Are you Dr. Douglas's assistant? Why didn't you tell me last night?"

"I'm not his assistant exactly." Mac cleared his throat. He reached out a hand, "Hi, I'm Dr. Macon Douglas. I know I should have done that last night, but…"

Katie couldn't believe it. This had to be some crazy joke. She stared at his hand and back to his face, her brain failing to register what had happened.

Oh, hell, I slept with a client. Well, technically there was no sleeping involved.

It had been one of the most passionate nights of her life and it was all a farce.

Katie's jaw tightened. "So you misrepresented yourself to me so you could get into my pants."

Mac moved closer to her, but she took a step back.

He held up a hand. "It wasn't like that at all. At first it was a joke with Timothy the bartender. But then, well, I enjoyed your company and I had a feeling if I told you the truth that would be that."

Katie's nostrils flared, and her fist tightened ready to punch his nose so hard it would go out the back of his head. She forced herself to take a deep breath as she stared at him for a full twenty seconds, working hard to keep her temper under control. When all was said and done, he was a client and she had to be respectful. It was the only thing that kept her from kicking him in the nards and shoving a fist in his nose. She didn't like being made a fool of, and he'd done exactly that.

When Katie didn't speak, Mac reached a hand out to her again, but she shook her head.

"Katie, please. I felt such a connection with you last night. I know what I did was wrong, but to be honest you didn't disclose that much about yourself, either. We talked about our families, but never what we did for a living."

He could explain the situation as many ways as he wanted. She wasn't sure she could ever forgive him. Best to focus on the case, and try to forget the night before.

Yeah, like that's going to happen.

Katie pulled her shoulders back. "Dr. Douglas, do you have the voice recordings and copies of the letters involved with your case?"

"I... What?"

"The threats, do you have copies? Or did you give everything to the dean? I need to begin as quickly as possible so we can wrap this up." It was hard to sound professional while wearing giant green sweats, in addition to the whole being-humiliated thing, but she was a professional.

Damn him.

She'd have to put a dollar in the swear dog bank she had at home. As a cop in the Bronx her language had been colorful, but she'd been working hard on her abrasive nature so she didn't scare away the Stonegate clients. She'd bought the cute puppy bank to encourage her to clean up her mouth.

Mac stared at her as if she had two heads. "Do I need to repeat myself?" Katie asked, her tone clipped.

His enthusiasm deflated, and his eyebrows furrowed with concern. Good. It served him right.

"I have the originals of the two tapes and one of the letters. The dean has the rest."

"The rest? How long has this been going on?" She mentally checked the facts she had in her head. From what they'd been told by the dean, this had been happening for only a few weeks.

Mac cleared his throat again and moved toward a file cabinet. Pulling out a folder, he handed it to her. "The calls began about six months ago. The letters about two weeks ago, and to be honest it's nothing. Scientists run into this sort of thing all the time. It's nothing to be alarmed about."

Katie didn't believe that. "What do you mean it happens all the time?"

"Those of us who work on government-sponsored projects get threats all the time. The work is secretive and highly classified. People assume it's weapons of mass destruction, and that pushes them to do all kinds of things."

"That's the most ridiculous thing I've ever heard," Katie said. Though she had no doubt there were people in the world who would do exactly that. It was insane to threaten someone without having any clue as to what they were really working on.

"I assure you I'm speaking the truth." Mac acted as if he were offended.

"I don't doubt the validity of what you're saying, Dr. Douglas. I was calling the people who would do such a thing ridiculous, not you."

"Oh," he said.

She took out the plastic gloves she kept in her bag and slipped them on her hands. Opening the folder, she read the letter carefully.

"Stop your research or die!"

The words had been typed. She sniffed the paper. It had been printed off on a printer. Excellent. That was her first lead. "I'll need to take this and have it tested in our lab," she told the professor.

"I don't know what good that will do, Katie. My fingerprints are all over it."

She shook her head. "I'm not worried about prints, though I'll have them check for those, too. I want to find out about the ink. If I know the source of the ink, that gives me the type of printer, and the watermark on the paper is easy to trace."

After placing the paper in an evidence bag, she pulled out the flash drive with the calls on it. The dean and professor had digitally recorded the messages, which made it easier for her. Normally she'd pop it into her computer, but she couldn't do that.

"Do you have a computer I can borrow? My laptop is down." No reason to explain her idiocy to the man.

"Sure."

He reached under the table and pulled out a laptop. "You can use this as much as you want. We have two extras in the lab."

"Thanks," she said, not bothering to look up. She waited for the computer to boot up and attached the flash drive.

The voice was mechanical, and she knew immediately the caller had used a cheap synthesizer. The message was the same as the one on the paper.

"This person isn't very original," she said. Her office had the equipment to separate the voices, and there was a good chance they would be able to tell her in a matter of days if it were male or female and what kind of accent.

"I agree with you." Mac sat on a stool at the end of the long steel table. He'd been watching her carefully while she worked, and it took everything she had not to look up at him. As mad as she was at him about his deception, their night had been unforgettable. At least the bulky sweats hid her perky nipples tight with the need for Mac's touch. "That's why I don't think it's that big of a deal."

"I have to disagree. This, along with the accidents, makes me think we're dealing with individuals or a small group who mean you harm. The threats are escalating, and that's never good. You need to take these seriously. I have no doubt these people want you dead."

4

MACON HAD LOST HIS MIND. It was as simple as that. This pint-size pixie told him someone wanted to kill him, and all he could think about was kissing her soft red lips. He'd had to sit down on the stool to keep her from seeing the hardness under his jeans, caused by the way she pursed her lips when she was thinking.

The woman was an enigma. One minute she was pure sex, the next a professional detective. He wasn't sure which one he liked best. Everything about her was sexy. Though he didn't think this was the right time to tell her so.

The emotions playing over her face when she'd realized what had happened the night before had been surprise, anger and then something he couldn't identify. He had a feeling she used that look when she had criminals under interrogation.

He'd royally screwed up. Still, he wouldn't change the night for anything. In fact, he'd do just about anything to make it happen again. Unfortunately, it would take a great deal of coaxing to get her to acquiesce. Katie had a tough side, and forgiving him would be difficult for her, which made him want to try all the more.

She'd listened to the recordings again, her face a mass of concentration. What was it about her that had him so tied up in knots?

The last thing he needed in his life was a complicated woman, and Katie was certainly that. He didn't have time for someone nosing into his life, especially with curves that— No. He needed to get rid of this woman and get back to work. As soon as he thought the words, he knew there was no way they were true. He wanted her again, and he wasn't ready to let her go just yet.

"You weren't what I expected." She glanced around his laboratory.

"What do you mean?" He was more than curious about that statement.

"To be honest, I expected the elderly professor type."

"Sorry to disappoint you," he said with a smile.

She didn't return it. Yes, she was one tough woman.

"Tell me again why you and the dean are keeping Scotland Yard out of this? Seems to me that would be the first place to turn."

Mac frowned. "We can't risk it right now," he said. "As I mentioned before, this is highly classified research. The cops would want to snoop into my work, and I'm at a crucial point right now. I can't afford someone accidentally leaking information. The dean didn't want to involve the police in order to protect the university's reputation. He knew I wasn't going to call anyone because of the nature of what I'm working on. You and your company were the dean's idea."

"I detect some sarcasm in there," she said as she

popped the flash drive into another evidence bag. "The dean may very well have saved your life. As I mentioned before, these threats are real, and they will continue to escalate. It's important we find the culprits as quickly as possible before they can do any more harm."

"So what is your plan?"

"First, I'll send these off to the lab. We'll have results in a few days. I could send them somewhere here, but my forensic lab at the agency is state-of-the-art and one of the best in the world. If there's something to discover, they'll find it.

"Until then, we follow up on leads here. I need a list of everyone who may have had access to your research now and in the past."

"You don't think it's someone who would have worked in the lab, do you?"

She wrote something down on the notebook she carried. "Dr. Douglas, at this point everyone who has come in contact with you over the last year is a suspect."

She couldn't be serious. "There's no way it's someone here at the university."

Peering up from her notebook, she gave him a wary look. "You're too trusting. Until we solve this case, no one comes into your lab except necessary personnel. With security like this, there shouldn't be much trouble while you work," she continued. "Have you had incidents in the lab?"

He shook his head. Every time she glanced at him, he wanted to reach out and touch her. Her auburn hair hung straight and shiny to her chin, and she shoved parts of it behind her ears. It was her voice, deep and filled with sex, that made his groin tighten even more, and his lungs struggle for air. There was a slight overpronunciation of certain vowels. He found it fascinating.

She snapped her fingers in front of his face and he realized he'd probably been staring at her like a cat after a canary. "Can you focus a minute and answer my questions? I need information. Has someone tried to hurt you here in the lab?"

"No, and they are not *incidents.* Unlike the dean, I do not believe what happened to me is related in any way. I have a long history of unfortunate mishaps. I have a tendency to bury my mind in my work and I don't take notice of the world around me. I am a complete cliché and fully admit to being an absentminded professor. And unfortunately, I'm often in the wrong place at the wrong time. I consider it a quirky trait. The dean finds it bothersome."

She grinned slightly at that as her pink fingernail tapped a distracting beat on the steel table. "So you weren't mugged a block from the university and run off the road twice in the last two weeks?"

Before he could answer she held up a hand. "And there were phone calls to the dean's voice mail. Both making comments that promised physical harm should you continue your research." She crossed her arms over her chest.

He guessed if one were to line up the events in such a way, it might look as if something was going on.

"Yes, those things did happen." Macon cleared his throat.

"Why don't you let me decide what's the best course of action, then?" She turned away from him. "The car accidents took place near a summer home? Correct? And you were mugged where?"

"About a block from my flat." The woman was determined. He'd give her that.

His eyes followed her as she circled the lab. She was one of those people who found it difficult to stand still for more than a few moments. He could tell by the way she constantly moved or fidgeted. She glanced out the window as if she was searching for something. Then she returned to where he sat.

She started to speak and was interrupted by a large gurgling sound. Her olive-skinned cheeks turned a delightful shade of pink.

Macon glanced at his watch. "Let me guess—you skipped breakfast."

She bit her lip. "I was busy solving some problems with work this morning."

That meant she hadn't eaten in more than twelve hours. He'd gone longer when working in the lab, but he knew it wasn't healthy. There was also this strange part of him that wanted to take care of her. The least he could do was give her a decent meal after what he'd put her through today.

"Why don't we head to the café at the student center?" He had started to mention a restaurant, but worried it was too early in the day for it to be open.

"I'm fine." Her tone was clipped and professional. She'd been embarrassed.

"Well, I could use a snack. I haven't had anything this morning." He shoved his laptop into a bag with a couple of notebooks. He'd been working on several equations when she'd arrived. "Perhaps I'll be better able to answer your questions with a full stomach."

"I guess if you're hungry, a break is okay. Though I had hoped to jump right in with the investigation."

Macon shrugged. "An hour for a meal can't hurt," he said. "And I'll keep my promise to answer any questions you might have."

Leading the way, he pushed in the code for the exit. Once they were through the two sets of doors, he pointed to another entry. "If you go through there, you'll find your clothing. I'll meet you out in the hallway in a few minutes."

She walked away, but stopped as her hand touched the doorknob. "What do I do with the sweat suit?"

"There's a hamper to your right when you walk in. The cleaning staff takes care of them for me."

"Thanks."

Even in the oversize sweats the woman oozed sex, and as she walked away he remembered his hands on her backside the night before.

Concentrate, Macon admonished. *Only days ago your purpose was to get rid of her. Answer her questions, help her to see logic, so by this time tomorrow she'll be gone.*

There was one problem. Macon wasn't sure he wanted their time to end quite so quickly. The woman in the next room was an interesting specimen and unfortunately he wanted to know everything about her.

5

KATIE HAD HER HANDS FULL with Macon. Staring out
the window of her hotel onto the busy London streets,
she tried to gather her thoughts. She still couldn't believe he'd kept his identity from her. What a fool she'd
been. If only she'd had a picture of him before that first
meeting, things would have been so different. She could
have beaten him at his own game—and missed out on
one of the best nights of her life.

Part of her wanted to kill him, or at least seriously
maim him for lying to her, but the other part wouldn't
trade the sex for anything. She would never tell him so,
but the way he'd stared at her as he made love to her
and the way they'd connected was something she soon
wouldn't forget. Katie took a deep breath.

But now was not the time to think about those incredible moments. The man was a client, with a rather
serious case.

Katie had no doubt someone had tried to kill him.
That he thought the threats were coincidences almost
made her laugh. Moving to the desk, she sat down to
go through the files the dean's office had gathered for

her. Flipping open the file with the police reports from the accident, she read through them.

The professor hadn't mentioned that the last accident had landed him in the hospital for two days. He'd sustained a concussion and minor lacerations to the face. But the doctors had been concerned about the head injury. He'd lost consciousness for more than thirty minutes and suffered a pretty good blow to the head.

She'd noticed a couple of small scars on his forehead and cheek. He'd healed quickly. Katie tasted blood in her mouth and realized she'd bitten down on her lip too hard.

You're making it personal. That's never a good thing. If you want to help this guy you have to separate the man from the amazing sex. Otherwise you're going to miss something and you're going to get him killed.

Katie cleared her throat and closed her eyes for a moment. If she wanted to help Mac, she had to stay objective. She couldn't do that if she was lusting after him all the time.

Tapping her right index finger, she again focused on the files from the dean. There was something there, something she wasn't seeing. She yawned and glanced at the clock. Only four hours until she had to meet the professor at the lab to escort him home. She'd given him explicit instructions to stay at work until she arrived. He'd laughed at her and wondered aloud how a tiny thing like her could protect him if there really was evil out to get him.

She'd smiled patiently and opened the laptop again. Typing in a URL, she'd brought up a site with training videos for the academy to show him how lethal she could be. There were several of them, and she'd pulled

up one of the advanced classes where she'd had to defend
herself against four opponents. In a matter of seconds
she had all four men, at least a foot taller than she was,
on the mat.

"How is that possible?" the professor had whispered.

"Training," she'd said confidently. "You don't
work in my field without knowing how to take care
of business. So when I tell you to stay put, I mean it.
Understand?"

He'd nodded, and then grinned.

"What?" she'd asked him.

"I didn't think it was possible, but seeing that made
you even sexier. That's seriously hot what you just did.
You're like a ninja woman."

She'd grunted and shut the laptop. The man was hope-
less. Promising she'd be back at six to take him home,
she'd left him in his office.

She had only four hours left. Four hours before facing
the man who stoked her desire with a mere smile. Why
did it have to be him? Any other man in the world, but
no, it was Mac. And damned if she didn't feel for him
more than she had any guy she'd ever met.

Four hours, and then she'd be on duty again until she
hauled him back to the lab the next morning. She still
felt jet-lagged. Her mind would be clearer if she rested
for a short while. She had a glass of water and stuck the
Do Not Disturb sign on the outer handle of the door.
Two hours of sleep and she could go another twenty-four
with no problem. She'd learned that at her former job,
too—a police detective was always on call.

After stripping, she snuggled down under the sheets
and did her best to clear her mind. It wasn't easy when

she remembered the last time she'd been in this bed it had been with Mac. The way he made her feel sent shivers down her spine.

The way he'd made her come so many times she lost count.

She pounded the mattress below her. "Damn you, Mac. Why did you have to complicate everything?"

MAC HAD A PROBLEM no equation would ever solve. He had it bad for Katie. He couldn't stop thinking about her. Images of their lovemaking the night before would pop into his head at the most inopportune times. In the middle of separating a strain of bacteria so he could study it under the microscope, he'd remembered how she'd laughed at the pub. That throaty, sexy sound made him instantly hard.

Then there was the way she'd eaten all her steak and salad, without a thought. Most of the women he'd dated ate only the salad, and half of that. For such a petite thing, she'd really enjoyed the food and the beer. He respected that in an odd way.

Scrubbing his face with his hands, he groaned. He had to get the woman out of his head and focus. Now was not a good time for him to be distracted. He'd made serious inroads with his research in the past six months and he was on the cusp of something big.

Katie was definitely a distraction of epic proportions. Three times after she'd left earlier in the day, he'd pulled up the videos to watch her fight. She was absolutely ruthless when it came to making a kill. The exact opposite of what he'd seen the night before when they'd been making love. She'd been nothing but hot sex and sensuality, from her sexy moans to the way she looked in those stiletto boots. He had to make love to her again. His sanity depended on it.

Mac walked away from the microscope and paced. That's what he did when he had a problem. The movement often helped him to focus. The work had to come first. The dean expected him to present his first papers in the spring, and there was no time for any sort of delays.

But Katie filled his brain.

"What are you, some kind of stalker?" He continued his walk. "She slept with you. You lied. And now she's pissed off. She wouldn't touch you again ever, especially with her rule about clients. And have you noticed that you're talking to yourself out loud?"

Mac stopped and stared at the ceiling. This was nothing more than a schoolboy crush. He'd get over it. He had to. Everything he'd been working on the past few years depended on it. That was it. The best thing he could do would be to cooperate with her so she could see that this so-called case was nothing more than his propensity for being in the wrong place at the wrong time. Then he could send her on her way and get back to work.

Yeah, right.

A KNOCK AT THE DOOR had Katie sitting straight up in bed wondering where she was. In half a second she remembered. London. The hotel. Mac. Jogging to the bathroom, she found the hotel robe and wrapped it around her naked body.

Someone knocked again.

"Just a minute," she said. It had better be important, since the person had obviously ignored the Do

Not Disturb sign. She glanced at the clock and saw that it was almost four. Rising on her toes, she squinted so she could see through the peephole.

Growling, she opened the door.

"I thought I told you to stay put. What the hell are you doing here?"

Mac stood staring, his eyes moving down to the swell of her breasts and back to her face, trying to hide a smile.

"Get in here," she said, yanking him into the hotel room. "We had a deal—I come get you at six and take you to your home. What's so difficult about that?"

"No need to be so cranky." Mac moved to sit down on the sofa in the living room. "I didn't know you'd be napping. I thought you'd be running around doing detective stuff."

"I was, but then I realized I had to get some rest so I could protect you tonight. Would you like to explain why you are here?"

"I had to see you."

Katie frowned, wondering what had been so important that he'd risk his life to see her. "Is it about your case? Did you remember something?"

"The case? Oh, yeah. The dean stopped by. He wanted me to give you these." He pulled a couple of files out of his backpack. "They're files about other programs that have been targeted at the university."

"Thanks. So this is it? It couldn't wait until six?" Frustrated, she pulled the robe tighter around her. "I need you to follow the rules, Professor, so I can do my job. That means doing what I ask so that we can both be safe."

"I took a cab straight here," he said by way of explanation. "I was never alone. It picked me up at the door of the science building and brought me straight here."

Katie looked to the ceiling, sighed and sat down again. "Anyone could have grabbed you on your way up here. The lobby at this hotel is crowded at four, because they have high tea, something the Brits seem to favor. I know this because when I checked in the desk clerk told me that I would need reservations, as the place was usually packed.

"There's the elevator, stairwell, any number of places someone could have been hiding, and you would never have seen them coming."

She threw her hands up in frustration. "I can't help you if you don't take this seriously. I'm good at what I do, but I can't do my job if you don't cooperate. It's that simple."

"I thought I was taking precautions by calling the cab. Normally I would have walked the twenty blocks or so. I don't see how someone could grab me in a room full of people or on a busy street."

She leaned forward, putting her elbows on her knees, and then remembered she was wearing the robe, so she sat back up. "You were mugged on a busy street a little over a week ago."

He shook his head. "That was kids acting tough. I gave them the few pounds I had and they took off."

"One of them hit you from behind with a bottle—your second head injury in as many weeks. They also tried to take the backpack you had on your shoulder, which no doubt had your laptop, right?"

He nodded. "I'd done some work at the pub."

"Right. Those kids were after more than your wallet. That was to keep you from catching on to what they really wanted. If that couple hadn't come around the corner when they did, the kids might have run off with it. Do you understand? Someone wants your research. I think we're dealing with people who know you and this is personal."

Something clicked in her brain. "That's it." She walked over to the files she'd been looking at before. All the crimes against Mac had happened at the same time of day. At the desk she rummaged through the files again.

"Let me guess, you have a pretty solid routine. You get to the university at the same time every day, and you leave at the same time. Am I right?"

He stood. "Yes, why?"

"It's simple. They know your schedule. It's either someone who is watching you, which will make them easy for me to spot, or it's someone close to you."

She couldn't help but smile. "I knew there was something I wasn't seeing earlier. If they were terrorists, they wouldn't be playing games. We'd either be talking about ransom or requesting your body back for the family."

"Don't pull any punches on my account." Mac's voice dripped with sarcasm.

"Oh, sorry. I was thinking out loud. I do that when I'm working a case. I apologize if I've frightened you."

"Not at all," Mac said. "I'm glad you've been able to put the dean's crazy ideas about terrorists to rest."

"No, he isn't crazy. Someone does want to cause you bodily harm. The dean is absolutely correct about that. But it isn't an outward threat."

Mac shook his head. "But none of this makes any sense. My friends don't have any reason to cause me harm. Most of them don't even know what I do. My colleagues at the university are professionals who have their own concerns. We are very pleasant with one another."

"Pleasant is an easy way to hide mercenary and evil," Katie said, her hands going to her hips. Her mind was on the case, but it didn't keep her from noticing the way his sweater hid his gorgeous abs, or the slight bulge in his pants her fingers ached to touch.

"The way I see it, someone is either jealous or desperately wants your attention. My guess right now is both. They ran you off the road, but you could have been more seriously injured had you been going any faster. The air bags most likely saved your life. We aren't dealing with a pleasant person. Trust me on this."

Mac's eyebrows drew together and she could tell he was upset. "Hell, I don't know what to think anymore."

"You said the files weren't the only reason you left early today. Why did you show up here?" she repeated.

Mac moved closer and reached for her hand.

Arousal pooled in her belly.

"I need you."

6

"WHOA, PROFESSOR." Katie stepped around Mac so she stood in the middle of the suite's living room. "That's not going to happen. I made it clear earlier this morning what happened last night was a mistake. I won't go so far as to say I regret it. The sex was great, and I never lie. But I have a reputation for being professional, and I'm not about to risk that because of you."

She was a tough one, his Katie. Yes, he'd already begun to think of her as his. He knew it was too soon, but he couldn't help himself. "So you're saying you don't regret it but it was a mistake. That's not giving me mixed signals at all."

Katie's arms flew around as she talked, revealing the curve of her breasts. Mac remembered how she'd tasted and how he'd teased her nipples into taut peaks.

"Professor, don't twist my words. It serves you no purpose. If we're going to move forward with your case we have to put last night behind us. It's the only way this is going to work."

Mac stepped closer. He craved the woman. She smelled of exotic flowers. "What is that perfume?"

Eyes widening in surprise, she looked at him as if she was trying to figure him out. That's when Mac realized his way in. She didn't respond well to his directness, even though she valued the truth above all else. Apart from last night, subterfuge wasn't something he usually enjoyed when it came to women. Katie was a special case, a variable he'd never come across before, and she didn't fit any equation he'd ever worked.

It was necessary to keep her on her toes and off guard. That he could do.

"It's magnolia," she said about the perfume.

Mac turned away from her and stared out the window. "I like it. I might pick up some for my sister. I'll have to find out where you get it."

The clouds had rolled in and the snow was so thick he could see nothing but white. He glanced down at his watch. It was too early for dinner. "I hear there's a terrific spa and gym here," he said. "I haven't been on a run in weeks. Would you like to join me?"

He turned back in time to see her eyebrows shoot up in shock. Whatever she'd expected it wasn't that. "I carry my clothes with me just in case I can work one in. I'll go change." Picking up his bag, he strode to the bedroom he knew she wasn't using. Yes, he would keep her on her toes, and she'd land right back in his arms.

KATIE HIT HER STRIDE around mile two on the treadmill. She had to admit the professor could hold his own. It was obvious from the lean muscles in his legs and his very unprofessor-like upper arms that he didn't spend all his time in the lab. His tight ass under those running shorts made her think nasty wonderful things. Things like curling her fingers around his shaft as she guided him into her. Unfortunately, she could look all she wanted but there was no more touching allowed.

She didn't know what kind of game he was playing, but he was up to something. When he'd said he wanted to sleep with her, her traitorous body had gone hot with need. Obviously she had the same kind of effect on him that he had on her. As much as she didn't want to admit it, the idea gave her a small amount of satisfaction.

Katie tried to focus on her breathing. This workout hadn't been the worst idea in the world. She usually spent an hour and a half a day in the gym or running. When she didn't work out, her body and mind felt sluggish. The run would help her stay alert on the job. It was also helping to get rid of some of the sexual tension that had crept up her shoulders when the professor was near.

Why did she have to lust after the one guy she couldn't have?

The man orgasmed you to Shangri-la and that's hard to forget.

Damn, Katie. Focus.

She chanced a glance to her left. The professor had hit mile three and had barely broken a sweat. Sensing she was looking at him, he turned his head and she became very interested in whatever was happening on the television.

One of the attendants walked up to her treadmill. "Excuse me, Ms. McClure. There's a call for you. Would you like to take it here? Or we have a private room to the left."

Katie slowed down. Who would be calling her here? She took the phone from him.

"Hello?"

"Mom, I've got her."

"Daniel?"

It was her brother. She could hear him talking to their mother before he could answer.

"Young lady, why aren't you answering your phone? I've been calling you for two days."

Katie sighed. Would she ever really get away from these people? "Hi, Mom, so nice of you to call."

There was a long silence on the other end of the phone.

"I'm out of the country on business, and I had a problem with my phone."

"And you couldn't call from another phone to let me know you arrived safely? Dear God, Katie, it was your first trip out of the country. Until you moved down south—goodness, I'll never know why—you'd never been out of the Bronx. Now you're Miss High and Mighty traveling the world, can't be bothered to call her mother."

"Ma, it isn't like that. I was—" She glanced over to find Mac watching her with amusement. Great, and she'd been lecturing him about how professional she was. Katie stopped the treadmill and walked around the corner. She wanted to keep an eye on the professor, since it was her job, but he didn't need to hear this particular conversation.

"Mom, you have to understand that when I'm working like this, I won't always have access to the phone. How did you find me here?"

"Why are you so out of breath? Were you chasing someone?" Her mother ignored the question. Knowing her family, they'd probably called the office when they couldn't get in touch with her. They were persistent if nothing else.

"No, I'm in the gym." As soon as she said it, she knew she'd made a mistake. She hit herself on the forehead with the phone, still able to hear her mother's rant.

"Oh, you have time to work out, but you can't let me know your plane didn't crash or that you hadn't been mugged."

"Mom, I'm a big girl and I can take care of myself. And honestly, the day a mugger gets the best of me— well, hell, he deserves my money."

Her mother sighed loudly on the other end. "Uncle Walter is sick again. Danny's taking him down to see that new young Dr. Ross. I want you to meet him when you come visit us."

The tongue-lashing was over and they'd moved on. She'd have to hear about everyone in the neighborhood. That part she really didn't mind so much. She missed her friends, the bar and, yes, even her family. Sometimes. This was not one of those times.

Every conversation she had with her mother these days began with a complaint about Katie leaving the family, and then it moved on to the young men she needed to meet. And it always finished with a good dose of if-you-never-meet-a-man-I'll-never-have-grandchildren guilt. Her mother was a good old-fashioned Italian woman and had it in her head that if Katie could meet a nice young man in the Bronx, she'd want to come home. Her dad, who had given her the Irish surname McClure, supported her decision to follow her career.

There was no way her mother would ever understand. Being the only girl in the McClure family came with the burden of procreation. Her brothers could run around and date as many women as they liked without getting serious and no on ever said a word. Katie didn't like the double standard.

Peeking around the corner, she checked on Mac, who was continuing his run. Hell, she had met a man. One who turned her inside out and made her body ache with need for him.

She'd certainly never met anyone like Mac in the Bronx. Katie loved the place, but she had no desire to return. Her life in Texas was far from perfect, but it was her own. Well, except for these daily phone calls, which even a dead phone couldn't keep away.

"If you work all the time, you're never going to meet a nice boy—Katie, are you listening to me?"

"Yes, Mom."

"Now, like I was telling you…"

The professor had finished his workout on the treadmill and moved to the weights. She watched as he lifted the weights over his head, the muscles so strong. Tensing, taut and powerful.

Her mother had paused, and Katie realized she hadn't been listening. "Uh-huh," she said, hoping that would suffice.

Her mother's prattling went on, but at the mention of the pub she paid attention again. "Your GJ threatened to sell the pub if your dad didn't start taking care of himself."

"Wait, what? What happened to Pops?" She and her father didn't always see eye to eye on the choices Katie made in her life, but they loved each other. There wasn't anything she wouldn't do for the man. She'd been Daddy's little girl, until she turned sixteen and decided she had a mind of her own.

"That's what I was telling you. He had a small episode and the doctors are worried about his heart. That's how we met that cute young Italian doctor I want you to meet. That man will have beautiful children, I tell you."

Katie rolled her eyes. "Mom, focus. What did they say about Pops's heart? Why didn't you say that in the beginning?"

"Angina. Said he has to cut the fat out of his diet. The doctor gave me a list of the foods he can eat, and I'm trying to figure out how to make his favorites healthier. It's not easy, mind you. Using lean turkey instead of sausage and beef to make lasagna is unnatural, but I'm doing my best."

Her dad was sick. Katie's big fear when she took the job in Texas was that as soon as she moved away something bad would happen to someone in her family. If GJ was upset, that meant Pops hadn't slowed down his schedule at the pub. He had plenty of help, but he was a man who liked to do things himself. He never leaned on anyone, and he was the strongest man she'd ever met—well, besides GJ. They were cut from the same mold, those two.

"Is he there?"

"Your father's resting. GJ insisted between one and four every day your father take a siesta. Of course it leaves me with three hours of walking around on eggshells while he sleeps. Don't know how I'm supposed to cook without clanking pans around."

Katie took a deep breath. "Maybe you could do some of the cooking down in the pub kitchen," she offered. "You always liked those ovens better anyway."

"Good idea, Katie girl."

Finally, some praise.

The professor had finished his workout and was headed toward her.

"Mom, I've got to go. I have a meeting in a half hour and I need to get a shower."

"Fine," her mother huffed. "But you call me or text Danny when you get your phone fixed so I know you're okay."

"I promise. Give my love to everyone."

She hit the off button on the hotel phone.

"Is everything okay?" The professor's T-shirt clung to those hard ab muscles she'd explored the night before. He had that sexy, earthy smell of a man who had just done something physical. "You looked worried for a moment."

"Fine. My mom was concerned because she couldn't get in touch with me, and my pop had some kind of angina attack."

"Is he doing okay?"

Katie pursed her lips. "The doctors want him to change his diet, which is going to be difficult with the way my mom cooks. She's hard-core Italian, but it sounds like she's adjusting. I can't believe she found me here."

"No matter how far we go, we can never get away from our moms. Mine calls every three days like clock-work. She worries I'm not eating right and sends a giant box of food each month, most of which I end up leaving in the faculty lounge at school because I could never eat it all."

"So, what's next on the agenda?" She reached for a towel from the basket and wrapped it around her neck.

"Do you need to get back to the lab, since you left early?"

"Dinner. I don't know about you, but after that workout I'm starving."

Katie could most definitely eat. She'd skipped lunch and had only half a muffin with Mac in the cafeteria earlier in the day.

"I hope you don't mind, but I took the liberty of ordering in room service." He glanced at his watch. "We have about an hour before it arrives, just enough time to get cleaned up."

The man was just full of surprises.

"When did you do that?"

"While you were changing to come downstairs," he answered.

Katie's eyebrow rose. Still, it would be easier to keep an eye on him in her room, and she did have that huge dining area in the suite. There was no harm in sharing a meal in her room, and it was safer than a restaurant, where she'd constantly have to search for suspicious behavior.

"Fine."

He gave her a wicked smile.

Yes, the man was most definitely dangerous.

7

AT THE DINING TABLE in her suite, Mac watched as
Katie eyed the last roll in the breadbasket. Knowing how
hard she worked out, he'd bet she was thinking about
how many miles it would take to run it off. As far as he
was concerned, she didn't need to worry about it. The
woman was perfect, from her perky breasts to her slim
legs that made her look much taller than her five-foot-
three frame. Several times during their workout he'd had
to think about cold showers and complex equations to
keep his pants from tenting.

In the shower afterward, she filled his mind. More
than anything he wanted her with him, the warm water
sluicing over their bodies as he pounded her against the
glass wall.

Cold showers. Complex equations.

He forced himself to think about the two things so
he could bring himself under control. At least he had
the table to hide the tent this time.

This randy teen behavior wasn't like him. Boners like
this hadn't happened since his crush on Mrs. Sullivan,
his eighth-grade environmental science teacher. Ah,

Mrs. Sullivan and her sweater sets. He hadn't thought of her in years.

Mac's plan to throw his bodyguard off-kilter had worked so far. She'd relaxed during their meal. Steering the conversation to music and movies, he'd discovered they liked many of the same things. Though she certainly had a propensity for violent films. Katie's choices were more along the line of psychotics on killing sprees. Unusual, since she'd been a cop for so many years.

That was the thing about her. She constantly surprised him. On the outside she was a beautiful pint-size pixie, but there was an innate toughness about her. Growing up with the two brothers she'd talked about probably had something to do with that, but there was more. He'd guess she'd been born with a tough shell, one that would be difficult to crack.

While he wouldn't manipulate her, he knew he had to keep her off guard. Otherwise, she would never give him a chance.

"You should take it." He motioned to the roll. "That way I can eat the rest of the trifle without feeling guilty." She smiled up at him as if he'd given her a gift, and took the roll.

Then she glanced at her watch. "I should get you back to your apartment."

He shrugged. "Why don't I just stay here?"

She folded her arms across her chest. "I wondered when you would get back to that. I've told you more than once, it's not happening again."

"What's not happening?" He played dumb so she would be forced to say it.

"Sex." Her eyebrow rose as she said it.

He had to bite back a smile. Clearing his throat,

he put his napkin back on the table. "I understand the word *no,* Katie. I wasn't suggesting sex. There are two bedrooms, and I thought I'd take the one you weren't using. In case you hadn't noticed, there's a blizzard outside." He pointed at the window and the twirling mass of white beyond. "I doubt taxis are even running tonight."

Turning in her chair, she glanced out. "Crap, when did that start?"

About a minute before he'd suggested they work out. The longer he stalled the worse the weather got. Before he'd left the lab he'd made sure his greenhouses were protected against what the forecasters were calling the worst blizzard in years. That's when he'd hatched his plan. He had a feeling if she came back to his apartment she'd feel too on guard. In her hotel room, she was on her turf. He'd taken the blizzard as a sign from the universe that he and Katie were meant to be together. Well, he knew that was stretching the truth, but he wanted to be close to her again and the snow was a legitimate reason to stay.

Katie stood and glared out the window. "I didn't know you had blizzards here."

Mac stood beside her and watched the massive white flakes float to the ground. "Honestly, it doesn't happen that often, but I've seen it shut the city down. Most of the time we just get a lot of cold drizzle, but the weather here is mercurial at best."

Her arms were still folded against her chest. "Well, it seems silly to try and go out in this," she said finally. "We can't risk getting stuck somewhere. Take the spare room. Do you have everything you need? I can run downstairs to the desk or see of they have a gift shop if you need something."

Mac had brought the bag he kept at the office, which was packed with a change of clothes and all his toiletries. The bag was so that he could leave at a moment's notice if something came up in one of his other labs, which were stationed around the world. He had greenhouses on four continents and he never knew when one of his experiments might need his attention.

His plants were important for the study of sustainable crops that some day could possibly prevent starvation as a result of droughts.

"I'm covered, thanks. Though I would like to send my clothes I wore today to the valet to have them washed and pressed. The same with the workout clothes, in case we are stuck here tomorrow."

That was a very good possibility. Mac had made sure of it.

"What?"

He walked to the television and flipped it on. "We should probably watch the news to see what they say."

"A winter storm warning is in effect for the next twenty-four hours..." stated the broadcaster.

Mac tried to look serious. "Now, that is unusual. They haven't had a storm like this in years."

"Kind of like back home," Katie murmured as she left his side. "It's cold and wet in the city during the winter, but we don't usually get much snow. If we do, it's usually a light dusting."

Mac nodded. "I grew up in SoCal, and we didn't get much snow, unless we went north into the mountains. I'm still kind of a kid when it comes to the white stuff.

And the university will probably call a snow day. They are a cautious bunch. They won't want to risk faculty and students slipping on ice."

"Damn," Katie said as she sat down on the sofa.

"Why are you upset? It's just snow."

"I need to meet with the dean, and I wanted to interview some of your colleagues on the list he sent over. This will put us behind another day."

Mac appreciated she had his best interests at heart. "That is tough. I know you're anxious to get back home."

If he hadn't been watching her closely, he wouldn't have noticed the change in her eyes. She wasn't ready to go home yet, but he had no idea why.

Hmm, yet another piece of the Katie puzzle.

"Well, since you'll have plenty of time to work tomorrow, would you like to watch a movie, or check out what's on TV? They have some great shows here, though much like home, weather like this will probably take precedence."

Katie tucked her feet under her. "Do you want to see if they have an action film? Maybe they'll have one we both haven't seen."

Mac picked up the remote with a big smile on his face. "Let's find out."

KATIE'S EVENING WITH MAC had ended up being relaxing. They'd watched last year's Dade McClain film and talked through it, just as she did with her family, making comments about the ludicrous stunts that would have killed any real-life cop. At the end, he'd yawned and said he was tired and had gone off to the bathroom. Only stopping to kiss her lightly on the cheek and telling her that he'd had a great evening.

As if they'd been on a date.

They'd had dinner and watched a movie.

It had been a date.

She laughed. She'd fallen straight into his trap.

That man.

She had every right to call him on his tactics, but that was probably part of his plan.

When he brought his clothes out for her to give to the valet, all he'd worn was a towel. It was if he wanted her to know that he would be lying naked just a few feet away from her bedroom.

Katie was quite certain showing off the man's abs was against some kind of law. No scientist should ever look that hot. They were supposed to be flabby and old.

Mac was neither.

Thinking of him made her tight with need.

This had to stop. She couldn't focus on protecting him if all she thought about was sex.

And there you go.

Now her mind was filled with the sensations he'd given her the night before. The way his mouth had taken her taut breast, his fingers driving her over the edge. The way he'd said her name as he—

Get it together.

Jumping up, she double-checked the lock on the door.

Then she moved to the terrace doors to check those.

Face it. This threat wasn't coming over a terrace ten stories up. Mac was safe, probably more so than if they'd gone to his apartment. No one downstairs could get past the security at the elevators or the stairwell without a key card, and their level had specially made cards.

She should try to get some rest. Leaving him on the couch, she headed for the bathroom. If he didn't go into the lab, she'd need to be on call all day tomorrow.

Katie brushed her hair behind her ears in frustration. If she tried to go to sleep, her mind would drift to thoughts of Mac.

No, it was better if she tried to stay awake as long as possible.

She turned on the television. The sound blared and she quickly turned it down. Picking up the files the dean had sent, she used her highlighters and pens to make a list of likely suspects.

For the next hour she was able to focus. Unfortunately as soon as she completed the task her mind wandered into dangerous territory again. She flipped the channels, but there wasn't much on.

Katie curled up, hugged her knees and tried desperately to think about anything but the man in the other room. It was insane—she couldn't get Mac out of her head. So they'd had great sex. People did it every day. Well, some people. She'd never experienced anything like it.

Jumping up again, she paced the room. If she hadn't been worried about leaving the professor alone, she would have gone to the gym to work out her frustrations on a punching bag.

"Katie?"

The professor's voice startled her, and she turned to face him. She thought he'd been asleep for at least an hour. He'd wrapped the towel around his hips, where it hung low. She followed the small patch of hair just below his navel.

"Yes?" Her voice sounded husky with need.

"Come to bed."

8

"I'M NOT HAVING this conversation with you again." Katie planted her feet firmly on the carpet. He liked her this way—her defenses on high alert, ready for a challenge. She didn't seem to notice it, but she'd pulled her shoulders back and her cheeks had turned a light shade of pink.

It was charming and hot all wrapped up in one beautiful package.

Mac stayed in the doorway, but held up a hand to stop the tirade he knew was coming.

"You're fired," he said softly.

The shock on her face was priceless.

"You—what?" Her words stumbled as she fought to understand what he'd said.

"I no longer want you to protect me. Now may I come to bed?"

Katie waved both hands. "Now, wait a minute. First of all—" she ticked a finger "—I was hired by the dean, so you can't fire me. And second, what do you think you're doing? We slept together once—a one-night stand. I realize that is a difficult concept for you, but there isn't going to be any more, Professor. You tricked me once, but it won't happen again."

Mac bit the inside of his lip to keep from smiling.

Clearing his throat, he ticked off a finger in the same manner she had. "First of all—" he repeated her words "—I'm more than happy to call the dean right now and tell him that I'm not happy with his choice of a bodyguard. That I would feel more comfortable with a male."

He knew that would get her.

"What a sexist!" Her voice rose several octaves, and the color on her cheeks deepened. "I can't believe you would say something so chauvinistic. I'm the best there is, buddy. I've been here twenty-four hours and without the opportunity to speak to even one person I've narrowed down the suspects to ten, out of the hundred or so the dean had listed. You saw what I can do in those videos, and you know you are perfectly safe with me."

Mac leaned to the right and crossed his arms against his chest. "I have no doubt my life is absolutely safe in your hands, Katie. I never said you can't do your job or that you aren't excellent at it. I said I want to sleep with you again. And I know you want me, too. You have rules about that, and I respect those rules and you. So I'm offering this compromise. You're fired."

"Argh. You are such an arrogant—"

"Jerk." He completed the sentence for her. "You value the truth above all else, right?"

"Yes," she said suspiciously.

"So stand there and tell me that you don't want me. That you don't want to experience what we had last night again, because it was special. You know it as well as I do."

She gave him a look of derision. "You have a very high opinion of yourself."

"No," Mac said seriously. "I have a very high opinion of you. Of the pleasure we can give one another. Answer my question, Katie. It's simple. Do you want me?"

"Professor, go to bed. I have work to do." She turned away from him, moving toward the French doors leading to the terrace. She pulled the handles, checking the locks. He'd already watched her do it once a few minutes ago. Though she hadn't noticed him.

"It's twenty-eight degrees outside, with the worst blizzard in recorded history. No one is coming in through the terrace. I get the feeling you're avoiding the question. Katie, tell me truth. If you don't want me, just say so, and I'll go back in my room without another word."

Katie pulled the curtains back over the glass doors. "Yes."

His body stiffened.

"Yes, what?"

She turned then. Her beautiful eyes focused on him. "I want you, Mac."

Before she could say another word he was across the room, but he didn't touch her. Mere inches from her, he kept his hands to his sides.

"You are in my every waking thought," he whispered. "My entire day was spent trying to think of anything but you. It didn't work. I don't do that sort of thing. I'm at a critical point in my research and for the past year I've been consumed with it. I'm ready to chuck it all just for one more night in bed with you."

"You confuse me."

He couldn't get a read on her emotions. Granted, he

wasn't always the best with that sort of thing, but he actually tried where Katie was concerned.

"What do you mean?" he asked.

He chanced moving a little closer. When she didn't back away he put his arms around her waist. When she didn't throw him over her shoulder, he took it as a good sign.

"Would you really blackmail me into sleeping with you?"

"I'm a desperate man, Katie. I need you."

She held her head away so she could see his eyes.

"I have a code I live by. Rules are important to me, Mac."

She hadn't called him Professor. He pushed her hair behind her ears. Then he leaned over and kissed her cheek. "I know, Katie. But I want you and if firing you is the only way I can make that happen, well, like I said, I'm desperate enough to try anything."

She reached up and touched his face. "If you fired me, who knows who the dean would hire next. I can't let that happen. Technically, it's better if I sleep with you so I know you're getting the best."

"Oh, I'm definitely getting the best." His fingertips trailed down her cheek to her chin.

Mac propped Katie up on the desk of her suite and slid her T-shirt over her head. "I say we start right here," he said as kissed his way up her neck. When his mouth reached hers, his hand thumbed her nipple into a taut peak.

Katie's body quaked with need, her mind reeling from her sudden change of plans where the professor was concerned. How could she possibly deny herself his touch? And if it was wrong, why did she crave him more than anything?

"I want it duly noted I'm doing this under duress and you left me no other options," she said breathlessly.

"Noted," he said before unhooking her bra and sliding the lacy bit of cloth off her shoulders. "You're so tough on the outside, but this lingerie…" He fingered the lace. "You aren't always what you appear, Ms. McClure." Mac tossed the bra onto the chair beside him and his fingers went to work helping her take off her pants.

"I'm exactly as I appear. There's nothing wrong with liking soft things against my skin." Her voice caught as his hand skimmed her stomach. The truth, though she'd never share it with him, was she had a secret passion for all things silk. She loved the way the soft folds of material melted against her body.

Once Mac had her completely undressed, he took her nipple in his mouth, his tongue laving circles around it.

"Ohhhh," she moaned. "You're making it really hard for me to stay mad at you."

"Baby, you have no idea what hard is. I wanted to take you right there on the table in my lab this morning."

When he nipped her nipple gently with his teeth, Katie's back arched and her hands moved behind her for support.

Mac gave her other nipple equal attention, leaving Katie squirming on the desk. The man had obviously studied a great deal of biology, because he knew exactly what to do to turn her into a heated, needy pile.

"Mac," she said huskily.

"Yes." His tongue slid down her stomach and stopped at her heat.

Katie forgot what she was going to say as his tongue kneaded her pink flesh. When he nibbled on the tiny nub there she nearly collapsed on the desk, and when she felt the towel slip from his hips she almost cried out in relief.

Soon he was inside her where he belonged, thrusting in and out, slowing at times and then speeding up. Katie wrapped her legs around him and shoved her hotness against his hard cock, dropping her head back.

"You're so beautiful," Mac said as he pumped her harder and harder.

His words blossomed in her heart and made her want him even more. No one ever called her beautiful. Strong. Capable. Never beautiful. The previous men in her life, not that there had been that many, weren't so free with the compliments. In one way or another they'd turned out to be selfish. She'd realized that even more the previous night when she and Mac had made love. It had never been like that for her before.

Mac paused.

"No," Katie groaned.

"Trust me, baby," Mac whispered as he turned her over on her stomach. Her ass in the air, she bent over the desk, hands grabbing the edge. He positioned her so that he could massage her breasts and used his fingers to spread her pink flesh so he could slide his cock back inside her. He penetrated even deeper than before and Katie groaned with excitement.

Everything became a blur. There was nothing like the glorious sensations their bodies made when working together. Nothing else mattered. One of his hands slid down to the nub as he pumped her, the other one still kneading her breasts.

"Yes," she cried. "Yes." The orgasm ripped through her like a rocket on the rise. Muscles limp, Katie couldn't breathe. Mac didn't stop, but he shifted her so she no longer had to support herself and rammed his cock into her so fast she could feel another orgasm building.

"Come with me, Katie," he begged.

She grabbed the edge of the desk, rocking against him as he plunged into her one final time.

They both gasped as the orgasms took them over the edge into heated bliss.

9

MAC HAD A BIG PROBLEM. Making love to Katie hadn't quenched his thirst a bit. He was inside her so spent he wasn't sure he could stand another moment. Yet he wanted her again—and again. What was wrong with him?

"I don't think I can move," Katie said softly.

The woman was everything. He didn't want to admit that to himself, but she was. Everything he didn't know he wanted.

Scooping her up, he gently carried her to the bedroom.

She wrapped her arms around his neck. "Am I out of your system?"

He drew his head back. "What?" Mac placed her on the bed. She couldn't have known what he was thinking. Then again, the woman was always full of surprises.

"I'm a good detective—we figure these things out. I wanted to know if it worked." She studied him with that intense gaze of hers.

"No. The experiment didn't go as I expected. I'm afraid we call that a null hypothesis with a type-two error." He sat next to her on the bed, but he didn't miss the sly smile that slid across her face.

"How about you? Did you get me out of your system, Katie?" Part of him wondered if she'd say yes out of spite, but he knew how her body responded to his touch. What they had together was far beyond anything he had ever experienced. It was as if their bodies came alive at the connection—atoms knocking against one another with incredible force.

"I always tell the truth, Mac. You know that."

He nodded.

"No." She took a deep breath. "No, you are still very much in my system. I think we should try your experiment again. Maybe it's one of those false positives or something."

"Or something." Mac grinned at her. "So you want to try it again?"

"Yes, but I need some of that wine we had with dinner. I'm thirsty." Her hand touched his cheek.

This woman was dangerous to his sanity. Making love to her again took no thought at all. Being with her was the most important thing to him now, and that scared the hell out of him.

He jumped up.

Coward. Mac was more than happy to oblige her desire for more lovemaking, but he needed a moment. One for his body to recover, though as soon as she'd said *again,* his cock had begun to harden.

"Wine it is," he said as he leaned down to give her a kiss.

Mac stopped by the bathroom to clean up. Staring at himself in the mirror, he frowned. He'd known this woman for less than twenty-four hours, and he was already attached. The man who never held on tight to anyone couldn't imagine letting this woman go. But he would have to, eventually. The only reason she was here was to protect him.

He thought about the way she'd moaned when he'd pounded her so hard he thought he'd break her, and she'd wanted more. His gut tightened at the thought of her skin under his hands, so soft and supple.

He was rock hard.

What have I done?

Mac gathered their glasses and the bottle of wine they'd had at dinner. As an afterthought, he picked up the chocolate-dipped strawberries.

Yes, she was here for a short time. They might as well have fun while they could. Once she solved this case, she'd leave and that would be the end of it. They'd both move on with their lives. Their experiment would be over.

Mac stood at the doorway and glanced at Katie's backside as she climbed into bed. Though there was absolutely no reason they couldn't continue pleasuring one another while she was here protecting him. As if his cock weren't hard enough already, the sight of her naked propelled him into the room.

No, their little experiment was far from over.

BUCKINGHAM PALACE was more grand than Katie had ever expected. She watched as the guard changed. Wrapping her arm around Mac's, she gave him a squeeze. The heavy snow had virtually shut down the city, so he didn't have to teach at the university. Most of the restaurants and pubs were open, but the museums and tourist places were closed. Claiming cabin fever, Mac had convinced her to get out of the hotel.

After trying to contact all the people on her list to see if she could meet with them, she'd given up on work. She hadn't reached a single person, so she'd left voice-mail messages all around London. She would never admit it to Mac, but she had cabin fever, too. She didn't like to sit still in one place too long.

Katie worried about his safety in public, but Mac told her he didn't mind being bait. If his stalker was stupid enough to go out in that weather, Mac was certain Katie would spot him. It had taken an hour and a half of cajoling, but she'd eventually given in.

"I can't believe you talked me into this, but I'm grateful," she said, watching the pomp and circumstance before her. Katie's mom had always been fascinated by anything to do with the royal family, so she took pictures to send.

"If I'm going to be bait, at least we can have some fun." Mac kissed the top of her head.

Katie wished he wouldn't joke like that. The man didn't take the threat against him seriously. The only reason she'd finally allowed the outing was that Mac had been right about the weather. The snow still fell at a steady pace and was three feet high in places. Not many people were out and about, and it was easy for her to keep an eye on suspicious behavior.

They'd taken the subway, or the tube as they called it here, to each of their destinations. So far they'd seen Westminster Abbey and Trafalgar Square. They'd even visited famous Beatles landmarks. That would please her father to no end. He was a huge Beatles fan—the back wall of the pub was loaded with memorabilia.

Mac's phone beeped. "We're in luck."

"Why?" Katie had no idea what his phone beeping meant.

"It's a surprise," Mac said as he took her hand. "Come on."

Katie followed him back to the tube. In the subway car they were alone, and he stole a kiss.

"Except for the last two nights, this is the most fun I've had since I came to London," Mac said against her lips.

"It's the most fun I've had in years," Katie admitted. For so long it had been nothing but the job. During her childhood she'd learned doing a good job gave a person a sense of accomplishment. Her dad would come home bone tired from his patrol, and she'd ask why he did it.

"I'm making a difference, cupcake. Daddy's helping people and making the world a better place for you."

While Katie's friend and favorite psychologist, Makala, would argue that she'd had no other choice than going into police work, Katie disagreed. Yes, she'd been born into a family of cops, but she'd never let them define her. Her goal was to be the first one in the family to graduate from college. She beat both of her older brothers in that respect. They finished their degrees on the job, but she'd whizzed through school.

Then one day when GJ made an offhand comment that with her quick mind and eye for detail she'd make a great police detective, the idea stuck with her. That was her next goal and she worked hard to achieve it, surprising everyone, not least of all herself.

"Hey." Mac put his finger under her chin. "I lost you."

She smiled at him. "I was trying to think of the last time I had fun like this, and I honestly can't remember. Sad, isn't it?"

"I have a hard time believing a beautiful woman like you isn't whisked off on fancy dates all the time." He had an incredulous look on his face.

Katie barked out a laugh and patted his knee. "You are a funny one, Mac."

"I meant it. I've been jealous the last forty-eight hours of every man who has had a chance to kiss you."

Katie's heart sped up. "That might be the sweetest thing I've heard, but you're still funny. Mac, I hardly ever date, and it almost never gets to the kissing part. I don't know if they're intimidated by what I do, or if I come across as too tough, but I seldom go on second dates."

"Now you're messing with me." Mac sat back and crossed his arms against his chest.

"I'm dead serious. In high school I dated Tommy Klein for three days and he kissed my cheek. Sister Clery caught us holding hands, and we had detention for three weeks. He wouldn't speak to me after that."

"Well, he was a dumb kid."

She'd eventually put Tommy behind bars for armed robbery, so she couldn't disagree about the dumb part.

"What about college?"

She shook her head. "I studied all the time, and worked at the bar to help pay for school. There wasn't time. Then on the job, it was the same thing. I was on call all the time. Every single time I went a date, I'd get called in. Guys don't like that. They'd never go out with me again. There was one guy I thought might be the one, but turned out he was a lying scumbag, who was more interested in how many women he could sleep with in a night. I found I was part of a long list."

"Well, then they're all idiots." Mac tugged gently on her hair. "I consider myself lucky, then, because you saved all those kisses for me."

Katie was about to lean in for another one of those delicious pecks when the subway car lurched to a stop.

Mac helped her up and they came out near the Thames. She didn't think it possible, but it was even colder here. The snow had continued to fall, and so had the temperature.

They half trotted to an enormous building near a bridge.

"This is London Bridge Tower," said Mac. "It's one of the tallest buildings in London and has spectacular views."

"Mr. Douglas?" A security guard at the door, who let them in, greeted them.

"Yes," Mac said.

"May I please see your identification, sir? You, too, miss." The elderly man smiled at them. Katie had left her bag at the hotel, but she'd slipped a small wallet into her jeans pocket.

Mac helped her take off her long wool coat so she could reach into her back pocket.

Once he'd checked their IDs he led them to the elevator. Stepping inside, he punched in a code.

"When you're ready to come downstairs, call from the phone next to the elevator wall and I'll come get you."

"Okay," Mac said. "Thanks."

They rode up for what seemed like several minutes.

"Where are we going?"

"A friend of mine has one of the first offices that went in here, and he arranged for us to visit."

"Oh." Katie had to admit she was disappointed. She enjoyed their time alone, and wasn't quite ready to share Mac with anyone else.

"What's wrong?" He must have noticed the worry on her face.

"Nothing. I'm excited to meet your friend."

Mac laughed. "Uh, no. The point of today is us spending time alone together. He's not here, and he let his staff have the day off. We have the place to ourselves."

Katie still didn't understand why this office was so important—until the doors opened. There was nothing blocking the view from the huge expanse of windows, and a snowy London made a picture-perfect postcard.

"Oh my," she said, her hand flying to her mouth.

Mac hugged her to him.

"Now I see why you wanted to come up here."

"That's not the only reason." He turned her body away from the windows to show her the office. There were huge video screens and toys everywhere. Giant robots, life-size ones, loomed like soldiers all around. There were slides, swings and a mass array of electronic toys and gadgets.

"What is this place?"

"The Kaba Toy Company," he said. "My friend Hunter inherited it from his dad and has turned it from a mom-and-pop shop, which was magical and still exists in Knightsbridge, into a multibillion-dollar corporation. They design toys for all ages as well as video games. It's a wonderland for a kid like me who didn't have a lot of toys growing up."

"Why?" She took his hand and squeezed.

"My parents weren't big on that sort of thing. If it wasn't educational in some way my parents didn't buy it. I had to hide my comic-book collection from them for years."

"Comic books?" She laughed. "You really are a geek."

"Hey." He gently chucked her chin.

She winked at him. "I'm kidding. I'm a fan of Batman myself. My brothers made sure I was well initiated into that world."

"Hmm. Batman? That says a lot about you."

"Like what?"

"Oh, I don't know. Caped crusader keeping the world safe—sound familiar?"

"I don't own a cape," she said quickly.

He grinned. "Come on, let's see what kind of trouble we can get into."

He guided her through a maze of desks to a huge glassed-in room with one desk and tons of toys. "This is his office," Mac said as he pulled her into the room. She noticed the center of the room spiraled down to a second floor below. There was a twirling ramp, painted in black-and-white checks that made her dizzy when she looked at it too long.

"Have you ever ridden a Segway?" The contraption was like a motorized scooter, only you stood instead of sitting.

Katie shook her head.

Mac climbed onto one of four machines against the wall. "It moves with your body. Here, climb on—this one holds two."

She did as he asked and he pitched forward. She

would have jumped off, but he held on to her and they headed down the ramp to the other floor.

Katie couldn't help but laugh—it was like a wild carnival ride. She couldn't stop giggling.

"This is a giant playroom for grown-ups, isn't it?"

Mac helped her off the machine. "Well, technically it's for kids, but grown-ups are welcome. They do testing in some of the rooms just off here, where children get to try out the new inventions. But for today, it's all ours. It's time to play." He waggled his eyebrows at her. "I know what I'm going to do to you in the bouncy balls."

Katie couldn't wait. She took off on a dead run and landed smack in the middle of the balls.

"Come and find me, Mac."

Katie, too, knew exactly what she was going to do to him when he found her.

_10_

IT TOOK MAC more than fifteen minutes to find her, then he kissed her senseless. Once he helped her out of the bouncy-ball contraption, they decided to try out the giant swings hanging from the ceiling.

"Now, this could be very interesting," Mac's voice teased.

Katie ducked away, but he saw her grin.

"Go play on the slide and tell me how you met Hunter."

Mac chose a big pogo stick instead. "At the pub, which funnily enough is where I've met most of my friends." He laughed. It was true. He spent most of his time at the university, especially those first few months. But he'd run into some interesting people at the Knightsbridge pub where he'd met Katie.

"Huh," she said as she sat on the swing and then spun it out of control. Mac loved watching her like this. The tension was gone from her shoulders and eyes, and the smile on her face was one of pure joy.

The sight made his heart do double time.

"And?" she questioned him.

"Oh, I was trying to find a last-minute gift for my nephew Taylor. He's the son of my second-oldest sister, Raina. She's a single mom, the best. Takes after my mom, who is pretty stellar even though she has something against toys that are just for fun. I actually have three sisters. I'm the only boy, and the youngest. They're all caring, loving women, who can't seem to keep their noses out of my life. It's like having four mothers, but I love them.

"Anyway, I had the laptop open at the bar and the guy sitting next to me happened to see I was on a page looking at toys. It was Hunter. We talked, and he took me around the corner to his parents' store. They hooked me up with the coolest remote-controlled helicopter, and my nephew still calls me King Uncle because I give the best gifts. Every time the holidays roll around or birthdays, I call Hunter and ask what's the latest and greatest.

"We play tennis two Sundays a month at the club with some other friends of ours. And his mom makes me come to dinner at least once a month. She can't actually cook, but she's a pro at finding takeout that tastes like homemade."

Katie laughed. "I don't know what I'd do without my friends," she said, but her voice had suddenly grown serious. "They keep me sane. Of course, we all work together, so we're always in each other's business. It's really not that much different than being home."

She crossed to the window and stared out at the scenery.

"Katie, what's wrong?"

She shook her head.

He put the pogo stick back where he'd found it and joined her.

"Tell me, please. Something I said upset you."

"No." She touched his arm lightly. "It isn't you at all. Well, it is, but not the way you think."

"I'm not following your logic." Mac truly was clueless.

"I can't tell them about you," she said. "They'd be so disappointed in me right now. We're pretty loose with the rules, but dating a client is a big one. And I've been here for two days and I've done nothing to solve your case. Well, I narrowed the suspect list, and I've left some voice mails for people at the university to call me back. I was able to get a feel from some of the students and faculty about how your role at the university is viewed.

"But I need to be out there doing the grunt work, instead of playing around here. What kind of detective am I? A guy makes amazing love to me, and I turn into a total flake."

Mac turned her so she faced him. "Give yourself a break. In the two days you've been here, you've done everything you could, given the circumstances. You worked all day, and kept me safe last night. And you're keeping me safe today. Think about it. I wasn't going to sit around a hotel room. Your job was to keep me safe, and that's what you're doing. It's quite logical. As for your friends at work, I've been thinking about them." He lifted her chin with his hand. "And I've deduced you have no need to worry anymore."

"Mac, you know what we're doing is wrong. It doesn't matter what business you're in, you don't sleep with your customers. Well, except for maybe one business, we are so not going there. I'm a detective, and it's my job to stay objective and to protect. End of story."

"Now, there you go ruining a perfectly wonderful day with misinformation," Mac told her.

Katie's eyebrows drew together. "What are you talking about now?"

"Let's set the record straight. I didn't hire you, Katie. I didn't ask you to protect me. I didn't ask you to take on my case. The dean did all that. And I'm sorry, but I'm not going to let what your friends think get in the way of this."

He kissed her then. Teasing her lips at first and then growing more passionate.

Katie put her hands on his chest and pushed away. "You're trying to distract me."

"Guilty," he said as he kissed her one more time. "Did you have fun today?"

"Yes. More than you know."

"Oh, I think I have a pretty good idea. But all this playing around has made me hungry."

"Do you ever stop thinking about food?"

He laughed at that as he guided her back to the Segway. "You'd be surprised how many times I forget to eat when I'm working," he said. "Though I think I've made up for most of those lost meals in calories alone the last two days."

This time she laughed, and the joy he'd heard before returned to her voice. "You know, I never had many toys that weren't trucks or superhero action figures," she said. "I can't remember ever playing anything but cops and robbers and stickball."

"You didn't have any dolls?"

She snorted. "Please, I had a doll one time when I was

really young. Liam used it for target practice with the BB gun he got for Christmas. She was so full of dents and tiny holes." She shook her head. "Nope, nothing girlie in our house ever survived."

Mac had always thought he took life too seriously, but Katie absolutely did. For however long she was here, he would make certain they had a good time together. The woman was due some fun.

"How do you feel about Chinese takeout?"

"I'm a fan," she said as they rode up the curvy path to the main office.

"It's a good thing I don't work here," Mac said. "I'd never get anything done."

"I'm sure after a while the novelty wears off," Katie said as they made their way to the elevator.

Picking up the phone, Mac called down to the guard station. Then they stood staring at the view again. Darkness had fallen while they played and the city lights twinkled. It looked like a magical world out there.

"You're probably right. Know what, Katie?"

"What's that, Mac?"

"You're one toy I'm never going to get tired of, and that is a fact."

She playfully pushed at him. "I'm a toy now? Hmm. I'm not sure how I feel about that."

Mac slipped his arms around her. "Hey, I'm careful with my toys, and I always play nice."

His mouth captured hers.

"No." She winked at him as the elevator doors slid open. "You don't play fair at all."

"I CAN HONESTLY SAY I've never eaten Chinese noodles in the bathtub." Katie rubbed her toes against Mac's thigh, as she used her chopsticks for another bite. Mac had insisted she jump into the bath to rid herself of her Popsicle status after walking in the snow. Then he'd brought the food in and told her to move so he could climb in.

"It's great, especially when you drop the noodles on your chest, which always happens to me," Mac said. "No stains on your shirt this way."

"Mac, have you ever eaten in a tub before?"

He laughed and shook his head. "Technically, no. But you have to admit it's a great idea."

"Okay, so we talked about my dating past, but I noticed you were quiet during that conversation."

"We're eating, in a tub, naked, and you want to talk about the women I've dated."

She pursed her lips. "Uh, yes."

Mac laughed. "Well, prepare to be bored."

Pointing her chopsticks at him, she encouraged him to continue.

"Well, I'll tell you about the high school years later. Suffice to say, there was only one girl, and it ended tragically."

Katie gasped. "Oh, no. I'm sorry. Was she killed?"

Mac guffawed. "No, she dumped me, but it's still too painful to talk about. I need to know you at least another day before I can share that story."

Katie rolled her eyes as she took another bite.

"In college I was going after multiple degrees, though I did manage to spend most Thursday and Friday nights in pubs and bars. There was a six-month period when I thought I was in love with Shelly Cramer and she sort of felt the same way, I guess. She had a chance to study abroad the next semester, and to be honest, I stopped writing her. Did I mention I was busy with school? Now that I think about it, I was a total geek. Let's just say if there were encounters, they were brief and not terribly memorable."

Katie laughed. "I have a hard time believing that. For a scientist, you're pretty creative."

Mac's brows furrowed with confusion. "What does that mean? I'm supposed to be boring because I work in a lab?"

"Now, don't get defensive. To be fair, I haven't met many scientists, but I can honestly say I'm pretty sure you aren't the norm. Most of the doctors and smart guys I've met are buttoned-down nerds."

"Katie!"

"I'm speaking from my own experience. Are you telling me your peers are as hot, sexy and sexually creative as you are?"

Mac glanced up at the ceiling and back at her. "You think I'm hot and sexy?"

Katie couldn't help but giggle. "You are front-cover-of-a-magazine sexy."

He pretended several silly model's poses one right after the other.

She laughed so much she had to put her food down on the ledge by the tub.

"So if I was a model would you still make love with me, Katie McClure?"

"Macon Douglas, I'm not sure I can keep my hands off you no matter what you do for a living."

"That's funny," he said seriously.

"What?"

"I seem to have the same problem where you're concerned," he said as he climbed out of the tub.

"Hey, where are you going? We aren't finished with our noodles."

"Oh, I have something much more tasty in mind," he said, scooping her up and wrapping a towel around her.

"Dessert?"

"Mmm. Yes." He nibbled her ear. "The tastiest treat I've ever had in my life," he said as he whisked her off to the bedroom.

11

THE NEXT MORNING, they entered the building and went through security, Katie was careful to watch everything around her. A few students said hello on their way to the classroom, and Mac always gave them his winning smile.

He genuinely seemed well liked by everyone they came in contact with, and she began to question her hunch about someone at school being the culprit.

"Mac?" A dark-haired man with a comb-over hairstyle and a lab coat stopped Mac in the hallway outside his classroom. He was about five inches shorter than Mac and a good ten years older.

Katie stood back so that she could observe without being overt about it.

"Phillip, good to see you made it out of your lab. We were beginning to think your project had eaten you alive."

Katie wondered what the man could be working on that could eat a human, but then realized Mac was joking.

"You're one to talk." Phillip gave him a quick smile.

"You got me there." Mac took the file folders the man handed to him. "Did you get those reports I sent you about the drought-resistant behavior of B1 and B2?"

The other man nodded. "That's what this is." He pointed to the folders. "I made some notes for you about certain bacteria you might want to try in the test trials."

"Ah. Good work here," he said as he flipped through the papers. "I appreciate the time you took to look this over. I know how busy you are."

"No problem," Phillip said. "Well, I've got to get back to the lab. I'll see you at the party later?"

Mac nodded, and as he turned to the classroom door he didn't see the strange look on Phillip's face. But Katie did. She made a mental note to check out the professor. Could be he was worried about something unrelated to Mac, but her gut told her she should check him out.

Katie had decided to observe one of his classes, since this was a teaching day for him. Maybe she'd pick up on something the students said, or the way he interacted with them. Back in the States students had done everything from pipe bombing teachers to egging their houses over bad grades. She wouldn't put it past someone to do the same, especially in a high-stress environment like this university, which was known for its excellence in academics.

Katie searched for the best vantage point to observe the class. Making her way up the stairs, she sat on the last row of the seats. With her jeans, jacket and knit cap no one would suspect how old she might be. Hell, there were times when she was still carded in restaurants in Texas.

The students filed in—noisy at the door, but as they reached their seats there was silence. They opened their notebooks and wrote down what Mac put on the white board in front of them. Earlier, on the way to the university, he had told her that he was one of the few professors who didn't allow laptops in the classroom. He found the finger tapping distracting, and half the time they were chatting with friends online instead of taking notes. He liked his students fully engaged. There was respect in the room—she could feel it. That made her curious. The absentminded professor obviously had some fans.

Mac busied himself writing things on the board while the kids settled down. Today he wore a cream-colored cable sweater and jeans, again making him look like a male cover model. If Katie were in his class, she most certainly would have a crush on her professor. Okay, she knew she was way past the crush stage.

In all, there were about twenty students. He'd said this was his largest class. Freshmen. Most of the professors hated teaching the underclassmen, but Mac told her he liked getting the young minds before they became too jaded about science. He saw this as his opportunity to bring them into his world.

A pretty blonde walked in just as the class was starting. She stood by the professor and tried to talk to him. He gave her a thumb motioning for her to sit down. When she turned toward the seats, there was no mistaking that expression. She was furious.

Katie chewed on her thumbnail, curious what that was all about. The girl huffed into her seat and slammed her books on the desk. She saw one girl turn and roll her eyes at her friends. The girl's lips read "Drama Queen."

Katie smiled, but had to find out what Mac had said to the girl to make her so angry. Pulling out her notebook, she wrote down the color of the girl's clothes and hair, and made a note to ask the professor.

Mac moved to the front of the long table he used as a desk in the front of the classroom.

"Good morning. I hope you did your reading for today. We have a great deal to cover before we get to your review on Friday. Let's talk about population density and food production."

As he launched into his lecture she expected to be bored to tears. But that turned out to be far from the truth. He was passionate about his subject and the kids were into it. They asked questions. Those who were shy he'd draw in, prodding them until they became involved. The whole thing made her respect him even more. She was so caught up in what was going on, she almost forgot her job was to observe.

The only person he didn't actively engage, and who didn't bother to participate, was the young blonde.

Katie's mind went to a bad place.

What if they have history? Would Mac date someone so young?

She and Mac had had a glorious two days, but what did she really know about him? In truth, he hadn't shared any more than she had, preferring to live in the moment. Pulling out the laptop that had arrived along with her new phone, she opened it and tapped the keys—gently, to keep from disturbing the class.

The computer had a satellite card, so she didn't have to worry about the university's wireless codes. The

Stonegate Agency used a specific satellite company for security reasons. Opening the databases they used for research at the office, she typed in Professor Macon Douglas.

His file came up. He'd done undergraduate studies at Harvard and moved to MIT for his graduate work, where he'd earned three separate doctoral degrees. She did a home search and discovered he had one in Surfside, California. That was where he grew up with his mother and father. And three sisters.

Interesting. He'd mentioned the mother of his nephew, but she'd forgotten there were more sisters, that he'd grown up in a houseful of women. That might explain why, even though he was a bookworm of a professor, he still had a romantic side.

She'd grown up with brothers, so she could relate. That was probably why Mac was so good at getting his way with her. All those women—he'd had a lot of practice in the art of persuasion. His résumé read like a Who's Who list. He'd met with diplomats around the world. There were even pictures of him with presidents in the U.S. and numerous dignitaries around the world. The man had certainly made a name for himself.

The research he worked on was top secret, but she perused several journal articles written about how universities around the world had wooed him. Mac had been wanted by the best.

The class was wrapping up and she needed to ask Mac about the blonde. Something about the girl didn't sit right with her. Stuffing everything into her bag, she made her way down the steps.

The girl took her time loading up her gear as if she

were waiting for the classroom to clear so she could talk to the professor again.

The girl hadn't noticed Katie, so she slipped behind a small partition that stuck out on the third row to watch what would happen next.

"Professor?"

Katie saw Mac's shoulders tense.

He shook his head. "Megan, I'm not going to change my mind. I'm sorry. I have two lab assistants and that's all I need right now. I tried to make you understand, but it's not going to happen." He erased the board without ever turning to face her.

"I know," she said sadly. "It's just, well, I'm worried about this midterm coming up. I was wondering if I could come by for some tutoring."

Mac still didn't face her, even though the board was clean. "Sara McKinley has set up a study group that meets Thursday nights here. She's the teaching assistant for this class, and helps me in the lab. That's your best bet for tutoring. But I'll be stopping by to answer any questions any of you might have."

She huffed. "I can't be here Thursday." Her nasally whine grated on Katie's nerves. "If you don't want to help me, I get it."

The girl hustled out the door, her shoulders hunched over the books she carried in her hands.

Oh. Crush. Katie knew what that felt like. She'd had a crush on one of her instructors at the academy. He was one of the reasons she'd done so well. Katie would have done anything to please the man.

"How about me, Professor? I could use a little one-on-one tutoring. Do you have time for me?" Katie teased.

Mac chuckled. "Yes, Ms. McClure, I will teach you whatever you wish."

"Who was that? The blonde."

His smile turned into a frown. "Megan. I turned her down as a lab assistant, but she's persistent. I made sure the application stated graduate students would be considered only, but she refuses to understand. Obstinate thing. She makes the other students uncomfortable at times. I seem to have one of those every semester."

"She has a thing for you, and she's just looking for a way to spend more time with you."

Mac scoffed, and the action made her laugh. "Well, I actually tried to fix her up with her classmate, Ian. He's a brilliant young man, and I have it on good authority from my TA that he's what the girls call hot. But Megan would have none of that. I see her everywhere I go. I don't want to say stalker, but sometimes…"

This time it was Katie who frowned. "You don't think she'd be angry enough to hurt you, do you?"

Mac's head popped up from behind the desk where he'd leaned down to pick up his pen.

"Oh, no. She's not the type. Annoying, yes. Attempted murder? I don't think so."

"You never know. We do stupid things for love," Katie said. She made a mental note to do some checking up on Megan all the same. Crimes of passion were the number one cause for murder in… Hell, in most of the world.

"So what's next?"

"I need to work in the lab for a few hours, and then I have a faculty party tonight at the dean's home. I don't suppose I could talk you into being my date?"

She sat on the edge of the desk. "Actually, I have to be there no matter what. While you're in the lab, I think

I'll see if the dean is in. I don't think he'd appreciate me asking my questions during his party."

Mac agreed. "He does these silly theme parties. For morale, he insists. But I think he has a thing for dressing up in costumes."

Costumes. Yuck. Katie hated that kind of thing. "What's tonight's theme?" she asked, praying she didn't have to find some awful outfit before the party.

Mac pulled an invitation out of his backpack.

He snorted.

"What is it?" Katie was afraid to know.

"Cops and robbers."

That she could do.

Mac's phone rang.

"Hey, Hunter. Tonight? Sorry, I've got a faculty party."

Katie remembered Hunter was the toy guy. She pulled out her phone to check messages, but she couldn't help but listen in.

"Yes, as a matter of fact I do have a date." Mac laughed. "Yes, she's gorgeous."

Katie's cheeks grew warm. No one said those kinds of things about her. Dependable, maybe, but never anything close to gorgeous.

"I probably won't be able to play tennis Sunday, but maybe next week? Tell your mom and dad I said hello."

Mac hung up and stuffed the phone back into his pocket.

"You play tennis?" Katie crossed her arms against her chest.

"A couple of times a month and usually with Hunter.

In the summer we also play soccer, though they call it football here. Do you play tennis? We could—"

"Not really my thing." She cut him off. As much as she would like to play all kinds of games with Mac, she was here to do a job. "I'm off to talk to the dean."

"Oh, well, I'll see you later, then."

Yes, he would. Katie couldn't get those words out of her head. *She's gorgeous.*

She might just take a little extra time with her makeup tonight.

12

THE DEAN PLANNED his parties down to the last detail. The foyer and formal living and dining areas of his huge town house in Notting Hill were dressed to look like an old-fashioned American police precinct. Faculty members stood around trying to look as if they were having a good time. Some were dressed as police officers or criminals in prison jumpsuits and stripes.

At every single function there was at least one idiot in the crowd who drank too much and said impossibly rude things. Usually it was some poor fool up for tenure, who knew he was doomed.

Thankfully, the fool had never been Mac. Though a few of his colleagues were swilling cocktails so fast, the party was sure to be lively in less than an hour.

Tonight Mac was on his best behavior. Katie had lectured him about keeping a professional distance at the party, especially in front of the dean. There would be no sexy moves on his part. She'd made him swear on the Bible in her hotel room. Standing next to her without touching her proved to be the hardest thing he'd done in a very long time.

He'd worn jeans and a T-shirt with a leather jacket, which was about as robber as he was willing to get. Katie, on the other hand, was the hottest cop he'd ever seen. He wondered how criminals had reacted to getting cuffed by her when she'd worked as a cop in the Bronx.

The woman was nothing short of perfect.

Only he could see the tiny line of tension around her eyes. She wasn't comfortable in this environment, but he couldn't figure out why. From the time they walked in the door, she'd been observing. He'd catch her checking out someone with a discerning look as if she were making mental notes of the guests. She spoke only when someone asked her something directly.

The dean approached their spot in the dining room, where they'd been talking about the food. There were piles of doughnuts, hamburgers and hot dogs.

The dean smiled. "I'm so happy you could join us, Katie."

For the most part Mac liked the man, and he certainly had no complaints about the funding he provided or the incredible facilities the university paid for that had been placed around the world under Mac's direction.

"Thank you, sir. I appreciate you allowing me to tag along with Mac." She gave him a sweet smile, and for a split second he felt a tinge of silly jealousy toward the older man.

"Yes, yes, well, who better than you to tell me if I've done this correctly." He waved to the spread on the table.

"The doughnuts are an inspired touch," she said. Then she placed a hand on his arm. "Remember, we don't want people to know about—well, you remember, right?"

She smiled at him, but it didn't quite reach her eyes. Something had happened in her meeting with him, but she hadn't discussed it with Mac. He had to admit he was curious. The dean seemed charmed by her, but she didn't care for him. Mac could tell by her cautious tone.

"So, what is our cover story?" The dean lowered his voice to a whisper.

"I'm simply a friend of Mac's," Katie said softly, but there was an edge to her words.

"Yes, of course." The dean put a finger to his lips.

"Katie's my friend visiting from the States," Mac chimed in. "She's a security specialist, and we met at a conference. Katie says it's best to stay as close to the truth as possible."

"Bloody good," the dean said. "Do you have any suspects in the crowd? I don't think anyone here is on the list I gave you." He glanced around the room. "I can't imagine the faculty would want to harm our dear professor, but as you said earlier, one never knows."

"I've been observing," Katie said, "but so far no one seems to stand out. Though I am curious about the woman in the jeans and red T-shirt. She keeps looking over here."

The dean started to turn around, but Katie touched his arm. "Don't look right now. She's doing it again. I don't want to call attention to the fact I've noticed she's watching."

The dean rubbed his hands together. "Oh, I feel like one of the detectives on those American television programs. Did I tell you I was fan of—"

"Yes." Katie cut him off. "Yes, you did tell me your favorites."

Mac coughed to cover his laugh. He also thought he'd better come clean with Katie.

"That's Caroline," Mac whispered. "We used to date."

The dean's eyes widened into giant pools behind his gold-rimmed glasses. "I didn't know you dated Professor Carson. Oh, but you needn't worry about her," he said. "She's one of our finest faculty members…well, besides Macon here, of course."

"Why didn't you mention her before?" Katie asked without turning to face him. She kept her eyes on Caroline.

"I'm embarrassed to say I'd forgotten," Mac said. "We went to dinner a couple of times and for coffee, but she's as anal about her work as I am mine. We never seemed to get past talking about our jobs."

Katie glanced up at him. Her eyebrow rose, and he knew he was in trouble. "It was a very casual arrangement. A few dates over a couple of weeks. I promise that was it."

He didn't know why he felt he should explain himself to her, but he didn't want her to misinterpret his relationship with the other woman.

"When was this?" Katie asked.

Mac shrugged. "I don't know. About six months ago?"

The dean rubbed his chin with his forefinger and thumb.

"What is it, Dean?" Katie had noticed the troubled look on the other man's face.

"We had a complaint from a female student during that time concerning Professor Carson."

"What was the nature of the complaint?" Katie crossed her arms in front of her chest.

"Well, it was unfounded. The girl had nothing to back up her claim, and the inquiry panel decided she was upset about her grade and made up the story. In the end after a good dose of questioning, she recanted her tale. As to the nature of the complaint, that is confidential information."

"Was it sexual?"

The dean's eyes opened in surprise again.

Mac knew Katie had her answer.

"So you think if Caroline was pursuing a relationship with Macon, then the girl was lying."

"My, you are good at what you do," the dean said. "It doesn't make sense she would risk her career and tenure to pursue a relationship with a student, especially if she were not of that persuasion."

The dean meant a lesbian, and Mac had to stifle a smile. To be honest, she could be a lesbian and he wouldn't know. He hadn't even held hands with Caroline. Other than the meals they'd shared, and their work at the university, they had nothing in common.

He had no romantic inclination toward the woman, and when he'd stopped calling she didn't seem to mind. He'd occasionally wave to her in the faculty lounge and she always returned the gesture. As far as he was concerned she was a cold fish. Mac remembered asking about her family and where she grew up, but she would steer the question back to her job.

No one understood that kind of intensity about the work more than he did, but he did occasionally like to leave the lab behind.

"I'm not sure she even knows I still exist," Mac said.

"Our labs are on different floors and she's always pleasant. But definitely uninterested."

"Hmm. She doesn't seem so uninterested tonight. I wonder," Katie said, her finger tapping her chin.

Those wheels were turning again, Mac could see.

Caroline moved into the other room, and Katie excused herself. "Gentlemen, I'll be back soon." She walked past the dean into the other room, following the same path as Caroline.

"Do you think she'll question her here, at the party?" The dean's face wore a horrified expression.

"No, sir. She's a professional, and as you said, she's undercover tonight. She probably just had to go to the loo." Mac knew Katie was up to something, but he didn't want the dean interfering.

"I've been eyeing those hot dogs for a half hour, and I want to try one." Mac put an arm around the dean's shoulders and led him to the table. "Won't you join me?"

"Hmm. I haven't tried the food yet. My wife had it catered. Yes, let's."

They picked up their food, and Mac made a good show of enjoying every bite.

More than anything he wanted to be in the other room finding out what Katie was up to, but that would have to wait. She might be the detective, but he would be the one asking the questions later tonight.

"Mac, who is that beautiful woman you're with tonight?" asked David, who worked in the biology department.

"Yes, everyone is talking about her. Quite striking," interjected Phillip, whose lab was down the hall from Mac's.

"She's a friend of mine from the States." He remembered Katie telling him to be as brief as possible when someone asked about her.

"Well, if she's just a friend, then—"

"She's not available, David." Mac cut the other man off, irritated by David's interest in Katie. She was the perfect combination of femininity and strength, and she was his.

He'd never in his life felt so possessive of a woman.

It scared the hell out of him.

Phillip threw up his hands in surrender. "We were only curious, my friend. Did you get the other set of files I left in your box this afternoon?"

Always the peacekeeper. Mac appreciated the man's attempt to move to a new subject.

"Yes, thanks, Phillip. I didn't have a chance to review them yet, but I will. The numbers you sent over this morning were quite interesting. I'd like to talk to you about them tomorrow if you have some time?"

"Yes, I have a free lunch tomorrow."

"Excellent." Mac watched as both men glanced behind them.

He turned to see Katie making her way into a hallway.

Katie had bumped into his friend Peter, who was most likely telling her made-up horror stories about him. Mac needed to make his way over there before Peter scared her off. It was the way the man's sense of humor worked and if she didn't understand…

Katie laughed and touched Peter's shoulder. Mac felt the tension leave his neck. Katie wasn't big on touching, so evidently Peter had genuinely made her laugh. He should have known they'd be fast friends. They both had that dark sense of duty about them.

"She really is quite remarkable," David said.

Mac noticed Phillip putting a hand on David's arm.

"I'll see you tomorrow," Phillip said as he ushered the man to the other side of the room.

"He gets everything," David whispered to Phillip as they walked off.

Did he? When it came to Katie he prayed that was the truth.

KATIE WAS JEALOUS. There was no other explanation for the way she felt, which only made her more of an idiot. Mac had said he and Caroline had a few casual dates. The woman was tall, slim, blonde and beautiful. Katie hated her on sight. Neither Caroline nor Mac fit Katie's stereotype of what a scientist should look like.

What is this? Do they search for supermodel scientist types at the university?

Katie had a difficult time believing their relationship had never made it past dinner. Her first meeting with him had ended up in the best sex of her life.

She leaned against the wall of the long hallway leading to the ladies' room, and took a deep breath.

Had the same thing happened with Caroline?

It made Katie sick to even contemplate the idea of Mac with another woman.

Oh, Katie, you really care about this guy.
Damn.

Katie couldn't fall for Mac. Not only was he geographically undesirable, but they came from different worlds. He was a brilliant eggheaded scientist, and she was a cop through and through. They had nothing in common.

That wasn't true. They'd had a blast the past two days, talking about everything from their favorite movies to food. For the first time in a long time, she'd let her guard down with a man. She'd stopped pretending and allowed herself to want more than a first date. There was no denying Mac had wormed his way into her heart. Being with him was easy, but it shouldn't be.

Forcing her thoughts away from the jealousy, she thought about Caroline.

The case. Was that why she was curious about Caroline? Her gut told her there might be something there, because of the timing. Mac's troubles had begun around six months ago. He'd received the first letter around the time he would have been dating the other woman.

Katie worried she was trying to create something out of thin air, because of how she felt. No, the timing of the problem with the student—her instincts told her that was key. There were too many questions surrounding Caroline. Had the woman dated Mac to throw attention away from her natural sexual tendencies?

She heard the door to the ladies' room open, and pushed away from the wall. Turning so that it looked as if she were staring at one of the paintings, she did her best to block the hallway.

"Pardon me," a woman said behind her.

Katie turned as if surprised. "Sorry, I was mesmerized by this painting. I don't know that I've seen anything like it."

"It is an original Koenig," Caroline said in her posh English accent, "and is one of the dean's favorites. He has quite the collection." She waved a hand down the hallway.

Katie had picked the painting randomly—the bits of black and white were mashed into odd figures.

"Interesting," Katie said, which was true. She didn't understand the painting, but she still found it enjoyable to look at.

"I saw you were with Mac. Are you dating?" Caroline cocked her head as she asked the question.

Well, that was direct.

Katie laughed. "No, just friends. I'm here visiting for a little while. Do you know him?"

The professor nodded. "We dated a few times, but he's not my type."

Mac was every woman's type. Unless she really was... Hmm. That was a real possibility.

"From what I can tell he works all the time—I don't know when he would have time for a relationship." Caroline frowned when she said the word *work*. Was there some kind of professional jealousy?

Katie had studied telltale signs for years, and that was definitely one of them. Caroline wasn't happy about whatever it was Mac did.

"Yes, I'm sure his research keeps him quite busy," Katie said. "And how about you?" Katie asked. "Do you work at the university or are you here with someone?" Katie had to play it as if she didn't know anything about Caroline.

"I'm a faculty member. I'm working on a special project, not unlike what your friend Mac is doing. Though I believe we are quite farther along than he is."

Oh, yes. There was definitely some professional

competition going on. There was a bite to the last sentence.

"I'm not very scientific minded, I'm afraid," Katie admitted. "Do you work with food like Mac? Although, to be honest, I don't really know what he does."

The professor scrutinized her. "I assumed you were a colleague of his."

Katie shrugged. "I am, I guess, but we aren't in the same business. You were telling me about your research." Mac had mentioned she loved to talk about work, so Katie steered her that way.

"I'm working on sustainable resources. I can't say much more than that, but it could change how we, and the Americans, support third world countries. We could make monumental strides in just a few years."

"Wow. That does sound important. I bet you must work really hard." She played dumb.

The other woman nodded. "I do. My work is my life right now. It's everything to me."

Katie smiled. "That doesn't leave much time for dating or fun."

"As I mentioned before, my work is important, but I do find time to date occasionally. I'm just discreet about it. The gossip around here can be nothing short of horrendous."

Katie remembered what the dean had said about the girl who'd made claims against Caroline.

"I'm sure. I've been getting strange looks all evening from some of the guests, so I can understand where you're coming from. I can't tell if it's because Mac doesn't date much, or if I'm American."

The woman gave a slight smile. "Probably a little of

both. Well, I should get back to the milling around."
She gave a quick wave and left.

Katie stood there a second longer. Something about
Caroline didn't add up. A thought niggled at the back
of her brain. A connection she'd made, but she couldn't
quite grasp it yet.

Since she was near, she decided to visit the ladies'
room and wash her hands before heading back to the
party. It would give her time to think.

From the outside, Caroline and Mac seemed as
though they would make the perfect couple. They were
scientists, dedicated to their work and passionate about
what they did.

Katie studied herself in the mirror. She'd worn a
white fitted T-shirt to go with her black pants, jacket
and boots. She'd worn more makeup than usual and even
she had to admit she looked okay. She pushed her hair
behind her ears and straightened her collar.

She needed to see those files about the claim against
Caroline. Caroline was mixed up in Mac's case somehow. Every time she'd said Mac's name, the other woman's mouth had gone into a straight line.

She didn't like him.

And who the hell wouldn't like Mac? Except for his
bullheaded, stubborn nature, the man was perfection.

13

AFTER DROPPING MAC OFF at his lab with the promise to meet him after lunch, Katie set her sights on the dean's office. Pieces of the mystery surrounding Mac shifted in her head, and her gut told her she was close to solving the puzzle. One thing Katie always did was trust her instincts.

"I'm sorry, the dean isn't in this morning," his secretary informed her.

Katie frowned. "I really need his help." Katie drummed her fingers against her thigh. "Do you know when he'll be in?"

"I can't say," the secretary replied. "He's in a Regents meeting and those can go on for hours. Is there something I can help you with, perhaps?"

Katie's tapping ceased. Yes, this might work better than her original plan, which was to badger the dean until he gave in to her request. "Uh, I'm not sure. Do you know why I'm here?" She lowered her voice in a conspiratorial whisper.

"You're helping with the case involving Dr. Douglas. I've been instructed to assist in any way I can."

Excellent.

"Well, I don't think this will be too difficult. I need a file about the complaint concerning Professor Carson last summer."

"Why would you need that? Surely you don't believe she has anything to do with the trouble."

"Confidentially," Katie said. "I do think their cases might be connected. And I understand the private nature of the file, but I've already signed everything the university asked me to for my security clearance, so I don't think it would be a problem."

The secretary was thoughtful for a moment.

Come on. You can do it.

"Imagine if you were the one to help me crack this case. The dean would be ecstatic. Maybe I could even talk to him about giving you a raise." Katie gave her a wink.

The woman waved her away. "No, you don't have to do that." She rolled away from her desk and stood up. Taking some keys from her drawer she went to a row of file cabinets.

"Do you need to make copies? That will take some extra paperwork on my part."

"Oh, no. I'll just look at them here, if that's okay." She glanced down at the nameplate. "Mrs. Gates, I really am grateful for your help. This file might save me hours of footwork."

"I'm happy to be of assistance." She pulled a file from the drawer. "Follow me and I'll show you to the conference room."

"Thank you." Katie gave the woman her warmest smile. She was on to something. Whenever she was close to solving her cases her stomach did a strange twisty thing, as if her instincts tipped her off that she was on the right track. It was how she solved her cases so quickly.

Her boss, Mar, at Stonegate swore Katie was psychic in some way, but she didn't believe it for a minute. She'd grown up around cops and looked at the world differently than other people did. That was all there was to it. She'd decided long ago that the stomachache was a mixed signal from her brain telling her to pay attention to the clues in front of her.

Katie hoped there was something in the file, because so far she was clueless. Mac didn't seem to have any enemies. Everyone loved him. She'd seen that at the party. People made a point of coming up and talking to him. He was kind and always introduced her. Even the dean was a fan, though she still disliked the man for not bringing in the police months ago to help with Mac's case. Then again, if that had happened, she might never have met him. Before her mind could go off on a Mac tangent, one that would send her racing back to his lab, she made herself concentrate on the circumstances so far.

The only person who'd avoided them was Caroline. As they'd moved through the party, she almost always seemed to be on the other side of the room. The woman's actions threw up a giant red flag for Katie, especially when she caught her watching them more than once.

"Here we are." Mrs. Gates opened a door leading into the conference room. "Would you like a cup of tea or coffee?"

Coffee wasn't a bad idea, but she didn't want to risk being here too long. The dean might have other ideas about her perusing the files and she wanted to get in and out as fast as possible. "I'm great, thank you. I won't be more than a few minutes."

"Take your time," she said. "Let me know if you need anything else."

After Mrs. Gates shut the door, Katie opened the file. The first few pages were forms required by the school. The young woman in question was only eighteen, but there was no name on the first few pages.

Then Katie opened a second file. There was the transcript from the deposition taken by both parties—the university and the girl's lawyer.

Initially the girl claimed Professor Carson had said that if she slept with her, she would give her an A. There had been some incidents of touching in the classroom, and according to the girl they'd shared several kisses in Caroline's office. When the girl refused to sleep with her, the professor had failed her on the first test. The girl said she'd passed it but the professor had changed her answers.

Katie rolled her eyes. If she had been involved she would have tossed the girl out then. Her story didn't add up. All the professor had to do was provide the test in question, and the handwriting could be analyzed, or they could have looked for excessive eraser marks on the paper. The girl's lawyer should have asked a proctor to readminister the test. Stupid mistakes all the way around.

In a second transcript the girl swore she had misunderstood the professor, and profusely apologized. She admitted she had a drinking problem, and that was most likely the cause of the misunderstanding.

Again, Katie wouldn't have bought it. This time the story really didn't add up, and it made her more suspicious of the professor. Had someone gotten to the girl? That's what it felt like. Katie had run into that more than once in her cases. Witness tampering was something she and the rest of the detectives fought against constantly.

At the bottom of the last page there was a signature from the girl. The paper stated all charges against the professor had been dropped, and the girl in question would attend alcohol awareness classes, as well as private therapy.

But it was the signature that made Katie gasp with surprise, and suddenly all the pieces fell together. She flipped open her laptop.

Something had told her the girl, Megan, the same one who had been harassing Mac, was involved with this case. Was it possible Megan had an accomplice? Perhaps it was this person who was the violent one, since Megan didn't seem inclined to be that way. Katie had a feeling they were looking for someone older. She'd stake her reputation on it.

The night before, she'd submitted various profile types into the database at Stonegate. The program had been designed by one of their programmers with the input of Katie and their resident FBI profiler and psychologist, Dr. Makala Liu.

Katie had inserted variables from the case into the system. During the night Makala must have been checking the files, because she had also added notes. Katie noted it was too early to call and chat with her favorite psychologist, but she read the notes.

"The attacks aren't original, and are almost formulaic," it said in Makala's comments. "This is a practical person, who isn't known for being the life of the party.

He or she lives simply, and has a daily routine that is followed to the letter. My best guess given the parameters is
a female. I'm seeing scorned lover here. Something has
made her step out of her comfort zone, and other than a
death in the family, a love relationship would be next on
the list, followed by loss of job or serious illness. Talk
with the client and see if he's had any disagreements
with a love interest in the last six months."

Several scenarios ran through Katie's head. Had Mac
had an affair with the younger girl?

Katie's stomach turned. Maybe she liked Mac too
much. Their whirlwind relationship had been so fast
and furious she'd never stopped to think about how it
would actually affect the case.

She'd insisted they keep it as professional as possible
during the daytime hours, but at night all bets had been
off. Her judgment was clouded.

*This is why you aren't supposed to get involved with
clients.* She cringed. Had she let her feelings for him
get in the way of the case? She didn't want to admit it,
but it was true.

First she had to talk to Mac. Standing up and walking
to his lab was one of the hardest things she'd ever had
to do.

MAC WAS PLEASANTLY SURPRISED when he saw Katie's
face on the security screen. He buzzed her in.

"Did you change your mind about the lab table?"
He'd remembered what she'd said when she left.

She glanced up to the camera.

"I'm not stripping again to come in there. I need
to talk to you and I'd appreciate it if you'd come out
here."

He wasn't the best at discerning human emotion, but even Mac could tell there had been a definite change in her attitude toward him.

"What's wrong?" he asked through the speaker.

"Dr. Douglas, I need you to come here, please. Is there anyone in the lab with you? This needs to be a confidential conversation."

Dr. Douglas. Crap. "I'm alone. Give me three minutes to put my samples away and I'll meet you in the conference room. It's the door to the right."

Washing his hands, he opened the door from the lab that led directly to the conference room. Katie didn't sit at the table. She stood with her arms crossed against her chest.

He moved to kiss her, but she held up her hands in a stop motion.

"Dr. Douglas, please sit down."

"Katie, why are you being so formal? What happened with the dean?"

She pulled out a chair across the table from him and sat down. He followed suit. Holding a pen over her notebook, she merely stared at him.

Mac couldn't read her face.

"I didn't speak with the dean. Not yet. I need to ask you some questions. It's important you answer truthfully. I'll know if you are lying. I'm good at that sort of thing."

Mac's brows furrowed. "Why would I lie to you? I can't give you details about my work, but other than that I'm an open book. You know that."

She sighed. "No, I don't. Listen, this is important. You need to put whatever mistakes we made these last few days behind us, and answer my questions."

"Mistakes?" How could she say something like that about their time together? Mac admitted he hadn't known her long. Still, he'd come to care for her.

"Yes. I should never have given in to you that first night. It's not your fault. I have a weakness where you're concerned. One I readily admit. Unfortunately, I'm afraid it's over now. I've come to my senses."

"The hell it is." Mac stood now. "I don't know what's happened, Katie, but we are most definitely not over. What could have made you say these things? You're acting like some cop, not the woman I—" He'd almost said the word *love*.

No, it couldn't be that.

Katie held up her hand. "Please, stop. I need you to sit down and answer my questions. The faster you do it, the quicker we can be done with this."

Mac didn't know if she meant their relationship or the case.

"Fine." He sat down again. "I'm sitting. Please ask your damn questions."

Katie leaned forward with her elbows on the table. "Have you ever dated or slept with one of your students? Specifically Megan, the girl I observed in your class yesterday?"

How could she ask him something like that? "I've never heard such a ridiculous question, and for the record, Ms. McClure, no. I haven't," Mac ended the words on a growl.

He thought he saw her shoulders drop, but her face gave no indication if she were relieved or if she believed him.

"Dr. Douglas, I need you to be honest with me. What you tell me is confidential, but I have to know the truth before I question Megan. I'll be talking to her in front of the dean, and if she says you had an affair we are going to need to take preventative measures."

Mac glared at the ceiling. "Let me get this straight. You think I slept with Megan, and yet you still want to protect me so the dean doesn't bring me up on an inquiry."

"Yes," Katie growled.

"May I ask why you would want to protect me? The dean is paying your fee, so shouldn't your allegiance be to him?"

"Technically, he pays the fee, but he made it clear from the beginning you are my client. And yes, when you signed the papers allowing us to investigate your case, one of the clauses is we protect you no matter the outcome."

"Katie." Mac clasped his hands in front of him to keep from banging the table. "The only woman I've slept with in the past five years is you. As I may have mentioned, I've been consumed with my work. I've been on the occasional date, never with a student. Never."

Mac sat back in his chair and crossed his arms against his chest. Fury pounded through his veins, causing his muscles to tighten and face to heat. He couldn't remember the last time he'd been so angry. He felt as if Katie had betrayed him in some way. Yes, the logical side of his brain told him she was only doing her job, but it hurt that she would think him so low and despicable as to sleep with a student.

"Do you have any idea why Megan, or anyone in her family, would want to cause you harm?"

Mac glared at Katie. "Megan doesn't have the sense to find her way into the classroom most days. She may have a crush on me, but she's not the person behind these attacks. I know this is rude, but she doesn't have the brains for it."

He leaned forward the same way she had. "Now I'd like you to explain how the hell you could think I would do something like that?"

14

KATIE HAD ALWAYS prided herself on keeping her emotions in check, but it was difficult where Mac was concerned. He was incensed that she thought he'd slept with Megan. She'd never been more relieved in her life when she discovered Mac spoke the truth—everything about his posture, mannerisms and face told her that. So did her gut.

Still, she had to make sure. "Would you be willing to submit to a polygraph?"

Mac leaned back with his arms against his chest. "Right now I'm angry you'd even ask, but yes, if it were necessary I would agree to the test. I'm telling you the truth."

The man was furious with her, but she couldn't let her personal emotions get in the way. Oh, who was she kidding? She'd messed this one up from the get-go. It didn't get any more unprofessional than sleeping with the client. Katie had been consumed with disgust and jealousy, and had jumped to illogical conclusions.

Once she stopped being blinded by all the silly emotions, she could see from his body language that he told the truth. Before he'd leaned back in the chair, his upper body, arms and chest had been open to her. There hadn't been any unusual ticks or twitches around his mouth when he spoke to her, and he'd stared directly into her eyes, his gaze never wavering.

"Thank you for your honesty," she said.

"That's it? A thank-you," Mac said angrily.

"Yes. The questions had to be asked, no matter what you think. The girl allegedly had a history with a professor at this school. If you'd had an intimate relationship with her it would explain why she, or someone near her, is seeking retribution."

"You're talking about her problem with Caroline," Mac said. "That's why I steer clear. I was on the inquiry board. The dean insisted, or I would have had nothing to do with the mess. Her father made a huge endowment to the school, which is why she is here. She's a confused, flaky young girl. It's obvious she has an aptitude where her studies are concerned, because her grades hold up. But her behavior is bothersome. I suggested the dean expel her, but as is usual with him, he was worried it might bring adverse attention to the university. There was also the question of what would happen to the endowment. The dean is all about appearances. He couldn't have that."

"The incident was six months ago, but Megan is a freshman."

"She began at the university the first summer term," Mac answered. "Her only class was Professor Carson's. The inquiry panel decided Megan had developed an unusual attachment to her instructor, and created these fantasies. This happens a great deal when young people are away at school for the first time and haven't learned how to socialize yet. Unfortunately for me, it's my turn this semester. Lucky me."

"Did she know you wanted to get her expelled?"

Mac didn't bother to look at her. "I honestly have no idea. Since it didn't happen, I assume not. You'd have to ask the dean."

"I will," she said. "Well, thank you for your time, Professor. I need to speak with the dean now."

Mac moved quickly to block her exit. "I think you owe me an apology, Katie."

"I refuse to apologize for doing my job, Professor Douglas. Now, if you'll excuse me."

"No, I'm not going to excuse you. What is this? Why are you acting this way? It's as if you're another person."

"I assure you, Professor Douglas, this is who I am. The woman who spent the last few days with you is an anomaly. Perhaps since this was my first trip, I had the same problem as Megan. I developed an unnatural attachment to the first person I met."

"That's it," Mac said through gritted teeth. "You are not going to turn what we have and make it something ugly. I won't let you." He pointed a finger at her forehead. "I'm not sure what's going on in that brain of yours, but you're wrong, Katie. Our relationship is not a mistake."

"Relationship? Please. I've known you for a few days. There's no relationship. It was a casual fling, Mac, and now it's over. Excuse me." Katie's gut churned with the lies she told. No one had ever meant more to her than Mac, but she couldn't risk letting this go any further— even if he hated her. The idea tore at her, but she had to do what was right for both of them.

She moved past him and opened the door. This time he let her pass. Katie didn't like leaving him angry, but it was better this way.

Though she would never tell him, their time together was no mistake. As he had said, they had been some of the best days of her life. But once she solved the case, she'd have to leave. Better to make the break now. She also needed her focus. Questioning the girl was her first priority.

Katie pushed back all the emotions, especially the ones causing the tears to brim. She closed her eyes and took a deep breath before pushing the button for the elevator. Long ago she'd learned how to push the emotions down deep. A Bronx detective often came across some of the worst crimes humanity had to offer. To stay sane, one had to learn how to compartmentalize the events and make it a part of the job. Though Mac was impossible to compartmentalize, she had to try.

Katie rubbed the ache in her stomach, which was rivaled only by the one in her heart. She wished the idea of leaving Mac and London behind didn't make her feel this rotten.

WHEN KATIE EXPLAINED to Mrs. Gates her reason for wanting to see the dean, he was called out of his Regents meeting. The investigator warned him of her suspicions. He was disturbed and grateful at the same time to have some kind of lead on the threats.

"I should have expelled the young woman as Dr. Douglas suggested." The dean led Katie into his office.

Katie knew exactly why he hadn't expelled the girl, but she didn't say anything.

At the door he asked Mrs. Gates to check the girl's schedule and have her sent to his office.

"I'd appreciate it if you'd let me question the girl," Katie said. "I'm trained in these situations, and it might help her, even though I'm a stranger, to relate to a woman. I can tell you I don't believe she's in this alone. But we have to be very careful if we're going to get her to admit her accomplice."

"Yes, of course. I'll be here in observation capacity only. I appreciate your quick work with this. What was it that clued you in to the girl?"

Katie didn't want to confess she'd seen the file—no use getting Mrs. Gates in trouble for helping her out. "I observed her in the classroom with Professor Douglas. He tried his best to keep a professional distance, but she kept invading his personal space. She also asked for personal tutoring, even though he told her several times that there were study groups."

The dean shook his head. "He should have told me she'd become a nuisance. She's been warned. We were more than lenient after that last escapade. Luckily for Professor Carson, we were able to keep things quiet. That sort of thing doesn't help the adult in question, even if they are exonerated."

"Oh, so there is a link to Professor Carson," she said, acting surprised. "I wondered."

The dean smiled. "Mrs. Gates tells me everything, Detective. She sent me a note, so I'm aware you read the file, even though I'd warned you it was confidential."

Katie smiled back. "Well, subterfuge isn't my favorite thing, but it was necessary. I had the feeling the cases might be related."

"Dean, the student you asked for is here," said Mrs. Gates over the speakerphone.

"Send her in, please," the dean instructed.

The girl walked in, visibly upset. Her hands were shaking as she moved toward the dean's desk.

"Megan, please have a seat," the dean instructed.

The young girl eyed Katie before sitting down, her lips turning into a straight line.

Katie held out her hand, and the girl took it. "Hi, I'm Katie. I'm helping out with something and I wanted to ask you a couple of questions."

The girl looked from Katie to the dean. "She's American. What is this?"

The dean leaned forward to say something, but Katie held up a hand to stop him. "I'm here working a very special case."

Megan chewed on her lip. "What does that have to do with me? I don't know anything about a case."

Picking up her notebook, Katie wrote down the girl's name. When she glanced up, Megan was even more nervous. "Actually, Megan, I believe you do. Unfortunately, I think someone may be using you. Maybe someone who may even want you to take the fall for them."

"What do you mean?" the girl asked.

Katie cocked her head. "There have been some attacks on a certain professor, one you know quite well."

"Who?"

"Professor Douglas, your environmental science teacher."

Surprise flashed across the girl's face, then worry. "What do you mean someone tried to hurt him?"

Katie pursed her lips. "I can't give you specifics, but the last incident landed the professor in the hospital."

The girl shook her head. "No, I like Dr. Douglas. I wouldn't do anything to hurt him." She looked to the dean. "I know you think I'm crazy, but I'm not. I'd never hurt anyone."

The fear in the girl's eyes confirmed for Katie exactly what she'd suspected. This girl hadn't been the one to hurt Mac directly, but she might have knowledge of who did.

Katie reached across the chair and patted the girl's hand. "Stay calm, Megan. We aren't accusing you of anything, I promise you that."

The girl's eyes became wild. "Do I need to call my family's barrister? I swear to you I had nothing to do with this—" She stopped talking and sat back in her chair.

A strange look passed over the girl's face. "No, it couldn't be," she said.

"Someone asked you to do something, Megan. Who was it? And what did they want?"

Tears brimmed in the girl's eyes. "She told me that *he* was the one bothering *her*. That if I kept an eye on him and let her know his schedule, then she could avoid him. She promised to help with my expenses if I could get hired as his lab assistant. My dad is paying my tuition, but after what happened last summer, he made me move out of my flat and he's cut off all my charge cards. I'm a prisoner at home. She told me she understood and—"

"Who offered you money to spy on Dr. Douglas?" Katie cut her off. She could tell the person had played some serious mind games with the poor child.

"You aren't going to believe me if I tell you," she said, glancing at the dean. "But I swear I'm telling you the truth."

"I'll believe you." Katie pulled Megan's attention back to her.

There was a long pause. The girl took a deep breath and closed her eyes. "She'll just deny it again. I can't believe I fell for her tricks. I love her very much, and this is the way she treats me?"

She took another deep breath and let it out slowly. "We had a fight and she almost got me chucked out of here. I just wanted to show her she couldn't kick me around. That's why I filed the complaint. We made up months ago. When she asked me to keep an eye on him, I was trying to protect her. I thought he was trying to find out about her research or something. She's very protective of her work. I thought it was weird, but it's hard for me to tell her no."

This time it was Katie who was surprised. "Megan, open your eyes. I need you to say the name."

"Caroline Carson, my lover. She's the one who asked me to spy on Dr. Douglas."

15

THE AFTERNOON TURNED into a whirlwind of activity. Much to the dean's chagrin, Katie insisted Scotland Yard be called in so they could file formal charges. Caroline had tried to kill Mac. Justice would be served.

The investigators asked Katie to come to headquarters while they questioned Caroline. She'd expected them to ignore her once they had the facts, but she'd forgotten the power of Stonegate. Her agency had been involved in several high-profile cases over the years, and had garnered the respect of Scotland Yard.

Katie had to give it to Caroline—she held up under some rather intense interrogation. There was a moment when Katie worried they'd have nothing more than Megan's testimony, which would be thrown out by any decent judge after her problem with the school. All Katie had was circumstantial evidence, but it was enough to warrant a search of Professor Carson's home.

That's when the detectives made the discovery sealing the case. A neighbor had lent the professor his car, and was still angry she'd wrecked the bumper. The paint on the bumper matched Mac's car. The friend said Dr.

Carson had borrowed the car on the nights in question, and she'd given him money to get it fixed. He just hadn't had the time.

After that, Caroline was processed and had no chance of bail, since she'd nearly killed Mac on two occasions. When the officers asked her why she'd done it, she replied, "He didn't deserve the funding they gave him. That money should go to my work—it's more important. I could save the world one day." It was the dumbest excuse for attempted murder Katie had ever heard. Mac could save the world, too, and research funding certainly wasn't worth killing over.

The woman was obviously crazy. She had absolutely no remorse in regard to her attempted murder of Mac. If Katie hadn't been on the other side of the glass, she might have throttled her. The idea of someone hurting Mac was more than she could handle.

Katie wished she could put the case behind her, but something niggled at her brain. She'd missed something somewhere. All the pieces didn't quite add up, but there were two signed confessions from Caroline and Megan that proved otherwise.

You're trying to find a reason to stay.

Back in her hotel room, Katie packed her bag for her trip home the next day. Mac had left one of his T-shirts in the bathroom and she held it close, sniffing his scent. The look on his face when she'd left the conference room would haunt her. She wished they'd parted on kinder terms, but it was better this way.

She was curious as to how he had taken the news. It was cowardly, but Katie had asked the dean to explain everything, while she went to headquarters. In truth, she'd been in a hurry to catch a ride with the officers, but part of her was relieved she didn't have to see him again.

All she wanted to do was throw her arms around him and kiss the man senseless until he no longer remembered her harsh words from earlier in the day.

That's not going to happen.

Taking out the few clothes she had in the closet, she folded them and placed them in her bag. It was surreal—she'd be home in twenty-four hours. So much had happened. Every time she looked at the bed her stomach tightened with need as she thought about Mac's hands on her, and the way his touch sent shivers down her spine. The man's tongue—

Stop it. Think about something else.

Katie wondered what he was doing. Even though she'd solved his case, she wouldn't blame him for still being angry with her. However, she really had been doing her job when she'd asked those questions. She couldn't go into that interview with Megan without all the facts. Although she'd lied when she said what they'd done was a mistake and she had a feeling Mac knew it.

Placing the last article of clothing on top of the pile, she closed her bag. Her plane didn't leave until noon the next day. She planned to follow up with the investigators before she left this evening, and then she'd get to the airport early, to give herself extra time.

Katie flipped on the television and sat down. She tried to examine her feelings, something she didn't do often. But she couldn't get a handle on the way she felt.

"I get this way every time I solve a case," she said

out loud. "It's the letdown after the adrenaline rush. Perfectly normal." Pushing the off button, she stood.

A workout might help her burn off the extra energy. She unpacked and changed quickly. Just as she was about to leave, her cell phone rang.

"Ms. McClure, this is Roland. You helped me with the investigation this afternoon."

"Hi, Roland. I was going to come down and see you in a few hours to make sure we'd tied up all the loose ends."

"Yes, uh, I'm afraid we have a problem."

"What's going on?"

"There's been another attack on Professor Douglas. A hit-and-run. I'm heading to the crime scene now. I thought you might like to meet me there."

Katie's breath caught in her throat.

Mac. No.

"Is he…" She cleared her throat. She couldn't bring herself to say *alive*. Tears brimmed as she reached for her purse.

"The officers on scene say he's dazed but okay. He's being checked out now. It looks as though he was on his way to see you—he's only two blocks from your hotel. Witnesses say the dark sedan was behind him and he never saw it coming. Luckily he was near a post and the car was moving slowly. He took a pretty nasty fall."

"Give me the address and I'll meet you there."

Mac was alive. She inhaled and then blew out the breath quickly.

Someone had tried to kill him. It wasn't over yet.

Guilt assaulted her. She should have listened to her gut and followed her instincts. He could have been killed tonight.

She ran the two blocks to the crime scene. Roland was there already and he motioned her under the tape. She saw Mac sitting in an ambulance and wanted to go to him. He was pretty banged up, with a cut above his eyebrow and several cuts on his gorgeous mug.

But Roland guided her to the skid marks. "It looks as though the driver didn't see the post until it was too late. From what we understand Mac had just stepped past it when the car hit the post and then grazed him. As you can see, the skid marks are quite short, which means the vehicle wasn't going very fast."

Katie forced herself to focus on Roland's words, but more than anything she wanted to wrap her arms around Mac. He could have died.

That was something she wouldn't have been able to handle. It had nothing to do with him being a client, and everything to do with how much she cared about him.

"That doesn't make sense. If it were a hit-and-run, surely the car would have been moving much faster," she reasoned.

"Yes, it is a puzzle. The witnesses say the car was definitely headed toward the professor, and at the last minute it swerved, hit him and then sped away."

"What about the cameras?" London was known for having most of the streets covered.

"We'll have to check that, but two of the witnesses have given us the license. We're tracking it now."

"It hit from behind, but did Mac see anything?"

"I haven't had a chance to interview him yet. I wanted to wait until you arrived."

She glanced over at Mac. He was watching her with a wary look. He had to be disappointed in her. She'd almost gotten him killed. She'd failed to do her job.

"I'd like to speak with him now," she said, "before they take him to the hospital."

The investigator nodded.

As they moved closer Mac continued to watch her. She could feel her cheeks reddening.

"Mac, are you all right?" She put a hand on his shoulder. When he didn't shrug away she felt relief.

"I'm fine. I'd like to go home now."

The emergency tech shook his head. "We need to take you to the hospital, sir, for scans."

"You told me I didn't have a concussion and I told you, it was nothing more than falling to the sidewalk. My face and hands took the brunt of the fall."

"Mac, we should be cautious. You *were* hit by a car," Katie said, forcing herself not to take him into her arms.

"I've been through worse and I know my body." He pushed away from the medical team. "I'm fine, gentlemen. I appreciate your looking out for me."

He turned to face Roland. "You had some questions for me?"

Roland ticked off a list of questions and Katie listened to Mac's answers carefully. He hadn't seen the driver or much of anything, since he'd been hit from behind. When Roland finished his questions he turned to Katie.

"Are you going to resume his protection?"

"Yes. If that's all right with him?"

Mac shrugged as if he was indifferent, but she saw the look of anger in his eyes. He wasn't happy with her, and she couldn't blame him.

"If you need anything else from him, you can contact

me on my cell," she said. "Mac, are you sure you don't want to go to the hospital?"

"Yes," he growled.

She gave him a tight smile. "Roland, do you think one of your men could take us back to my hotel?"

The investigator waved over one of the other officers. "Take Ms. McClure and Professor Douglas where they need to go. Do not tell anyone where you are going and watch for anyone who might follow," Roland ordered. "In fact, take a roundabout way, so you can make sure no one is behind you. Understood?"

The officer gave a quick nod and ushered them to his vehicle.

In the backseat they sat in silence as Katie watched out the windows to make sure they hadn't been followed. "Don't drop us off in front—take us to the parking-garage elevator," she instructed once they'd reached the hotel.

The garage would be a safe place for the drop, and then they could take the service elevator up to her floor.

As soon as they were in her room, Katie dumped her purse on the desk.

"Would you like some tea or coffee? Are you hungry?"

"I'm fine." Mac sat down on the couch.

There was more silence.

Katie sighed. "The investigators are following up on the license. Hopefully, we'll have a lead soon. Do you know if Caroline was dating anyone in particular?"

He shrugged. "I spend most of my time in the lab, so I don't pay much attention to that sort of thing. To be honest, before that party the other night, the last time

I'd even seen her was a few months ago in the faculty lounge. If I remember correctly she was dining alone, as was I." He didn't bother to look at her, only stared straight ahead.

Katie bit the inside of her lip. The situation was intolerable. She'd messed up, but she couldn't stand the idea of him being mad at her.

"Mac, I screwed up. You could have been killed. Just say it."

He glanced up at her with an incredulous look on his face. "You think what happened tonight is why I'm mad?"

"Why else— Oh, this afternoon."

"Yes, Katie, this afternoon." He stood.

She motioned him back to the couch. "You were hit by a car an hour ago—you really should sit down. In fact, I'm worried about you—"

"I told you I'm fine and you're avoiding the truth. I'm furious that you think I'm the kind of man who could sleep with one of his students. You have to know the very idea is so abhorrent to me I can barely stomach it."

She did know it. *Now.* "Look, you're right about part of that. I could have handled it better. I jumped to some conclusions before I had all the facts. If I'd talked to the girl first, we would never have had that conversation."

"You really don't get it, do you?"

"What? That I should have known someone else was after you? That Caroline had another accomplice? That I should have listened to my instincts and followed up when all the pieces fell too neatly together?"

"Katie, I care about you, and why you wouldn't trust me."

"You should care that someone is still trying to kill you. I could have protected you tonight if I'd been smart enough to follow up. As for earlier today, well, I might have mentioned I haven't had the best luck with men. We've also had the conversation about my trust issues. I've never hidden the fact that I don't trust anyone."

"That's a ridiculous way to live your life, Katie. You can't spend the rest of your days worrying how someone is going to hurt or betray you. You'll end up bitter, never happy."

That stung.

"Let's face facts. I am always going to second-guess motives, be curious about what is going on around me and thinking the worst about humanity. I've been out there. I've seen what happens in the real world. You're so isolated and protected in your lab that you don't have a clue. And, Mac, you're gorgeous, intelligent and quite possibly saving the world. You aren't exactly Katie Mc-Clure dating material."

Mac frowned. "What does that mean?"

"It means you're too good to be true. So I was looking hard for an imperfection. I jumped to a conclusion I shouldn't have earlier. How many times do I have to apologize for that?"

"Katie, I don't want your apology. I want you to trust me. To know that I would never do anything like that, or anything to harm you."

She rubbed the bridge of her nose. "Mac, this will be easier if we—I…" She wasn't sure exactly what it was she wanted to say. "I need to stay objective, and I can't do that if we continue our, um, relationship. I fully admit that I care about you, but I still have a job to do. I have to keep my distance."

Mac scoffed. "You're impossible. I'm going to bed." He grabbed his backpack and headed for the guest room.

"Mac, it's only seven," she said softly.

"Yes, and it's been one long, awful day. Hopefully, the police will find out who was trying to kill me tonight, and you'll be rid of me for good."

Katie watched, speechless. Why couldn't he understand this was for his own good? She didn't want to be rid of him. In fact, it took every bit of strength she had to keep from running after him and begging him to forgive her.

She leaned back against the desk and stared out the window onto the terrace.

The police shouldn't be the only ones looking for his killer. Katie needed to find him or her before it was too late. Gathering up her files and notes from the investigation, along with the copies of the confessions and details from the police, she sat down at the desk.

The killer was somewhere in the files. She was sure of it.

16

MAC FOUND IT DIFFICULT to stay angry as he peeked in on Katie, who was asleep on the couch. She looked angelic lying there with her hair fluffed out on a pillow. The files she'd been reading long into the night were scattered around her.

Last night he'd had every intention of making things right with her, of showing her that he was someone she could trust. But his temper had gotten the better of him. The crazy thing was, he didn't even have a temper. Sure, he was frustrated when he couldn't work out a formula, but he couldn't remember the last time he'd even raised his voice.

You've never cared enough to fight for someone in the past.

That was true. Katie was worth fighting for, and he'd do almost anything to win her trust. But he understood that when it came to the tough private investigator, her trust was something earned. She wouldn't be manipulated or cajoled. He understood that now.

At least they had more time together. The circumstances surrounding the situation weren't the best, though. He couldn't imagine who was trying to kill him now. The past few days had seemed like some kind of surreal television episode. Nothing made sense anymore, except for Katie.

He'd known just by the look on her face that she'd felt responsible for the accident the night before, but she shouldn't have. Even the police had been fooled into believing the case had been solved.

Mac had a feeling she'd be anxious to get on the case right away, and he wouldn't keep her from it. But he also had to check on his greenhouses after the blizzard. Everything was temperature controlled, but one couldn't be too careful. He knew she wouldn't allow him to go off on his own, which meant he'd have to convince her to take at least half a day to run out to the country with him.

Katie's phone jangled and he stepped back into his room and shut the door before she could see him.

His body was stiff. Maybe a hot shower would loosen him up and give him time to think about how he could persuade Katie to believe that what had happened to him wasn't her fault. They'd never be able to move forward if she didn't stop blaming herself.

He'd help her with the investigation. In his line of work he was known for finding solutions to the toughest problems.

It's another type of equation, and when we have all the variables we plug in the facts. I can do this.

KATIE PULLED HER HAIR BACK in a short ponytail as she answered the door. Room service had arrived with coffee and the warm scent was so delicious she couldn't get to it fast enough. She signed the check and poured a cup for herself and one for Mac.

She stared at his door for a full minute before deciding she should knock. She'd never been a coward about anything in her life and she wasn't going to start now. She'd made some big mistakes the day before, and she'd owned up to them.

She tapped lightly on his door.

He didn't answer.

Great. Now what?

Maybe he was still sleeping. Or he might have a concussion.

She knocked again.

Still no answer.

She opened the door gently. He wasn't in his bed.

"Mac?"

"I'll be out in a sec."

She noticed his backside reflected in the bathroom mirror as he stooped to put on his jeans. He was covered in bruises.

"Oh, Mac. Are you all right?" Part of her wanted to go to him, but she knew that wouldn't do any good.

"I'm fine. A little beat up, but it looks worse than it feels, I promise," he said as he walked out of the bathroom. He grabbed a T-shirt off the end of the bed and pulled it over his head. "I sure could use some of that coffee I smell."

She stared at him and then turned away. She had to, in order to keep from kissing him. Mac was hurt and it was her fault.

He followed her into the living room, where she handed him his cup, her hand so shaky she almost dropped it.

He took the coffee in one hand and her hand in his other. "Stop it," he said. "I don't want you to blame yourself for this. No one saw it coming, least of all me. The only person I blame is the idiot driving the car… well, and Caroline. I can't help but think she had another accomplice."

Katie moved away from him and took a seat. "I've come to the same conclusion. Though I can't, from the information we have so far, figure out who."

Mac sat down across from her. "I can't help you there, either. I've been trying to remember if I've seen her with anyone else, but no one comes to mind."

Katie tapped her finger on the arm of the chair.

"Before we get into that, I want to apologize to you again," she said, her voice tight with nerves.

Mac leaned forward to speak, but she help up a hand.

"I should have trusted you yesterday when you told me the truth about Megan. I wanted to believe you, I promise you that. It's—it's my own issue and it's one I don't see me conquering any time soon."

Mac tried to interrupt, but she held up her hand again.

"No, please. Let me finish. I should have been there last night to protect you. My gut told me everything wasn't as easy as it all seemed, and I ignored it. I just don't seem to be able to see straight where you're concerned. I think it might be a good idea for me to bring in another detective, one who can be more objective."

That would be the best solution. Mac needed good protection and she was no longer the right woman for the job.

"Are you finished?" He eyed her warily.

She shrugged. "I've put in a call to the agency to see who is available. I also checked with Scotland Yard. They've talked with Megan again, but she didn't know anything about another accomplice. Caroline is refusing to speak."

Mac leaned forward on his elbows. "I don't want anyone else protecting me," he said.

"You—" Katie started to interject.

"It's my turn," he insisted. "I honestly don't want any protection, but if I have to have it, you're the only one I *want*."

The way he said *want,* there was no way she could fail to understand his meaning.

He still wanted her.

"This guilt you feel is just part of you, Katie, and there isn't much I can say to keep you from feeling that way. But you need to know that I don't blame you for anything. It makes sense why you had trouble trusting me. As much as it hurt when it happened, I've had some time to think about it. You'd only known me for a few days, and as you said that's one of your issues. I honestly don't know how I would have felt if the tables had been turned. So who am I to judge?"

Could he possibly be that understanding?

"I believe I can help you with the investigation. I'm good with problem solving if I know what kind of equation we're looking at. I won't hinder you in any way, but I would like to be involved. And I would appreciate it if you'd call your agency and cancel the arrangements to bring someone else in. Now, maybe you can tell me what else the police have discovered since last night."

He stood then and took her face in his hands. He kissed her lightly on the lips and then sat back down.

Katie was breathless.

She watched him reach down and pick up a file folder. He wanted to move ahead, and it was time she did the same.

"The car that hit you was a rental. They'd paid in cash and gave a fake driver's license. We do have a description from the rental owner. He's a white male between the ages of thirty-five and forty-five, professional looking with a slight paunch around the middle. They've got a sketch artist working with him this morning, but those don't always work out.

"The owner said the man seemed fidgety. The car was found in an alley a mile from where he hit you. No one seems to have seen the driver exiting the vehicle."

Katie scanned the photos Roland had sent to her via computer, her mind back on the case. "There's something that's been bothering me since we were at the scene yesterday."

"What's that?" Mac moved so that he could see the photos.

"Look at these skid marks and how they curve. I—I don't know. The driver wasn't going more than five miles an hour. If he wanted to kill you, well, he would have been going much faster."

Mac put his hand under his chin. "The angle is wrong, too. I was on the other side of the post. You might be right. I don't think he was trying to hit me so much as I stepped into him trying to correct the car at the last minute. And the light—look at that."

Mac pointed at the snow in the second picture. "Do you think he was blinded by the sun hitting the snow?"

"The glare on the camera is pretty strong, so that's a

real possibility. But if it were only an accident, why would he run? And the cash rental is highly suspicious."

Mac frowned. "I can't help you there."

Katie continued, "The witnesses didn't mention that the car seemed out of control. In fact, they thought he was heading straight for you."

Mac shrugged. "Yes, but if he couldn't see me because of the glare…"

She tapped her finger on the screen. "The pieces just don't fit. I wouldn't mind taking another look at the scene. Would you mind coming with me? If you don't want to, I can have one of Roland's men stand guard. He did offer."

Mac shook his head. "Actually, I need to run an errand and I was hoping you would come with me. I know you don't think it's too safe to go out, but this concerns my work and I really need to see something."

His lab was the most secure place for him, so that wasn't a bad idea. Then she could follow up some of the leads on the case. "I can get you to the lab and—"

"No," he interrupted her. "I do need to go to the lab later, but I also need to check on my greenhouses. They're about an hour and half from here."

That was a lot of time away from London, and she really needed to work on the case. She could send someone from Scotland Yard, but would they protect him as well as she could?

"Is it something that can wait until tomorrow?"

"No. I promise this is important. I need to make sure everything survived the blizzard. A temperature of five degrees one way or another can make a difference in the health of the plants. If we leave now, we can be back here by two. You can then take me to my lab and do whatever you need to."

Two o'clock wouldn't be that bad, and he seemed earnest about it being important. But they'd be trapped in a car for an hour and a half.

Oh, come on, the guy needed to check his plants. She could handle a few hours in a car.

Katie's gut said something completely different, but she chose to ignore it—again.

17

KATIE ALERTED ROLAND that they were leaving the city for a few hours, and then she called for a car. The driver was to meet them on the third floor of the parking structure. She still questioned whether they should be leaving town, but Mac reassured her. Evidently his excitement about seeing his plants had ultimately convinced her.

Mac put the car in Drive and followed Katie's instructions on what to do once they left the parking garage. They had decided he would drive so she could keep a lookout.

It was hard for him to believe everything that had happened.

Right now, though, he wanted to focus on Katie. If she had any idea how he really felt about her, she'd run away as fast as her gorgeous legs would carry her. He had to show her that they had something worth fighting for.

He'd seen the fear in her eyes. This was uncharted territory for him, too, but he refused to be fearful. Whatever the risk, it was worth it where Katie was concerned.

She knew him as some geek-head scientist. Mac needed her to realize there was more to him than his work. Albeit he was the first to admit his job had consumed him the past few years, that was about to change. His teaching and research would continue, but Katie would also be a part of his life.

While they were driving, she was making calls to her office, checking out the window every other minute or so. They hadn't seen another car for the past ten miles, but she was ever vigilant.

Time passed quickly and finally Mac pulled into a long drive, stopping at the gate. He rolled down the window to announce himself on the intercom. "Dr. Douglas and guest," he said.

The gates opened.

"Is this someone's home?"

"It was," Mac replied. "Sir Winston was kind enough to bequeath it to the university. The house was built in the early eighteen hundreds and is considered historically significant. The school uses it for a variety of functions. My contributions are there to the left." He pointed to a large glass conservatory.

"Holy cow. Look at the flowers."

Mac grinned. He hadn't met a woman yet who didn't love flowers. Even tough Bronx cops.

"Did you grow these?" she asked as they moved from the car to the door of the conservatory. The snow began, and he quickly slid his security card across the access eye so they could enter. Mac ushered her into the warmth of the building.

He watched as she closed her eyes and took a deep breath.

"This is heaven," she said on a big sigh.

Mac squeezed her shoulders. "I won't get too egg-headed on you, but we are growing these flowers in a variety of soils. Some of them are a part of my research."

"Are these snap peas?"

"Yes," Mac said, amazed that those were the first things she noticed. The peas were a key element of his research, and the reason he was so close to a major breakthrough. Maybe he couldn't tell her the specifics, but he could show her.

"But there's no soil, only sand." She glanced up at him, her eyes wide with surprise.

Mac shrugged.

"You—oh. So." She understood now. His research had everything to do with growing food in all types of terrain. It wouldn't be long before he could turn arid deserts into lush farms.

He held a finger to his lips and pointed to the security monitors.

She reached out and squeezed his arms. "Have I mentioned how amazing you are?"

"I'm not sure I can hear those words enough," he said as he took her hand and kissed her fingers.

They toured the rest of the conservatory as well as a couple of greenhouses. Every time he thought she might get bored, she'd grab his hand and beg to see more. They ended in the greenhouse where he grew a variety of roses and orchids.

"I thought the first place smelled like heaven, but this is a feast for my nose," she said as they strolled through the room. "I'm not sure how you ever leave this place, it's so beautiful. My mom would cry with joy over all these roses. We have a small backyard where she grows several varieties, but nothing like this. I'm a city girl, but I'm also a big fan of nature. That probably comes from watching too much Discovery channel with my brothers, and being so deprived of green spaces in the Bronx."

Mac took some shears and clipped one of the roses. "This is for you," he said as he gave it to her. It was a black red rose, with purple shading within the petals. Roses were his hobby. He'd been working on this one for several years.

"It's lovely," she said. "It looks like some kind of surreal painting of a rose. I've never seen anything like it. Almost too beautiful to be real."

"So you like it?"

She nodded. "I love it—thank you."

Mac smiled with satisfaction. "That's good, since I've decided to name it after you."

She lifted her face to his. "What?" Her cheeks turned the beautiful shade of pink Mac had come to love. "Can you do that?"

Mac laughed. "Yes. I usually give them numbers for names. But it only seems right that this one bear the name of my new passion. You."

Katie bowed her head.

Mac lifted her chin. "What's wrong?"

He watched as she took a breath.

"It's too much. I mean, you're naming a rose after me. You've only known me for a few days."

Mac took the rose from her and brought her into his arms.

"Katie, I don't want to scare you, but I feel like I've known you my entire life. Naming a rose after you is the least I can do."

She gently pulled on his ear. "Well, when you put it all romantic like that, makes it kind of hard for a girl to say no. Besides, what girl wouldn't want to have a friggin' rose named after her? My friends back home are going to be so jealous."

She took the rose from him and sniffed it. "I wonder if someone can make me a perfume from this thing. It smells like a garden in spring. I want to bathe in it."

Mac squeezed her to him. How in the hell was he ever going to let this woman go?

"I guess we'd better get back to the city, though I'd rather stay here with you."

She took the hand he offered. "My brain needed this. I feel like we have a fresh start for everything. I'm anxious to get back and talk to Roland and his team. They should have a sketch done soon."

Mac wasn't ready for all of that. He'd meant what he said about staying here with her. She was relaxed and happy, if only for a few minutes. He kissed the top of her head, wishing they could stay in the protective bubble of the greenhouses a little longer. He had a feeling it wouldn't be long before she solved the case.

Then she would be gone.

18

THEY WERE STUCK IN TRAFFIC just outside London, but Katie didn't care. For the life of her, she couldn't remember feeling so light and free as she had in those greenhouses.

When he gave her the rose and named it after her... well, it was the most romantic gesture anyone had made for her. Katie had seen a lot in her days as a police detective. It had hardened her against the world, forced her to put up shields she hadn't even known were there.

Seeing the world through Mac's eyes had changed that. The lightness in her heart was addictive and she craved more of it.

"Can I ask you a question?" They were stopped at a traffic light and Mac turned toward her. "Why did you leave your job as a cop?"

She chuckled. "What, you can read my mind now?"

He gave her a questioning glance.

"It's weird because I was just thinking about that."

"Why?" he asked.

Shifting in her seat, she faced him. "Today was... Well, I've been working so hard for so long that it was like coming up for air after being underwater for a really long time. I left my job four years in because I was already burned out. Grandpa Joe and my dad have been cops all their lives, but it wore me down. I don't think I realized how much until today."

"Huh. If you needed to get away from that kind of work why did you go to the Stonegate Agency? Seems like more of the same to me."

"No. Not at all."

Mac moved the car forward in traffic and they almost made it to the light that time.

"When I was a cop, most of what I saw was the dark side of humanity. Stonegate, well, it's been insanely busy, but we have really interesting cases—everything from corporate espionage to finding lost people. I'd say eight out of ten cases end up being incredibly rewarding. That sounds like a lame commercial, but it's true.

"My problem is I came down to help bring Mar, who inherited the agency from her mom, up to speed. She's brilliant, but was just out of graduate school. She hadn't done a lot of fieldwork and suddenly this entire multimillion-dollar business was dumped in her lap. She was drowning. There were case files and billing, and I was so caught up in helping her keep things afloat, my life once again became the job."

Mac squeezed her hand.

"If nothing else comes out of this, you've helped me to remember I need balance. I'm going to be an old woman before I'm thirty if I don't stop it."

Mac laughed. "Katie, one thing you'll never be is old."

She leaned across the seat and kissed his cheek.

"Thank you for that. So how does a hot guy like you end up working with flowers?"

He chuckled again. "You never hold back, that's for sure. Uh…" He turned the wheel and finally were on a street without traffic. "My family, I guess. My mom was a botanist who taught at the university near where we lived in SoCal. My dad was a corporate landscape designer. I kind of rebelled in my teens and decided I would be a rock musician. I even had my own garage band."

Now it was Katie's chance to laugh. "Oh, no. What was the name?"

"Black Satan." Mac rolled his eyes.

Katie couldn't imagine the man beside her in a band with that name. She couldn't stop laughing. Finally she caught her breath. "I remember you mentioning this before, but you never explained the situation. So, what happened with the band?"

"You know." He affected a cool rock-star voice. "We just couldn't keep it together creatively. And by that I mean the drummer was making out with the bass player's girlfriend behind his back."

Katie bit her lip to keep from laughing again. "And which one were you?"

Mac gave a dramatic sigh. "The bass. I caught them in my backyard out in the gazebo. I busted up his drum set pretty bad. He told my mom, and I was grounded for a month. Plus I had to work in her gardens and greenhouse for two months to help pay back the damage. Every minute was pure torture.

"Then one day, my mom showed me where she'd spliced two roses together and created a new one, and I was hooked. I became a complete and total nerd after that. Sold my guitar and used the money for science camp that summer. I was sixteen."

"What did your friends think about that?"

"Well, hell. I was sixteen. I didn't tell them about the camp. I made up some elaborate story about a family vacation. Lied through my teeth. But that camp set me on a new path. I finished high school in six months and went straight into university."

"Wow. That's awful young."

"Too young, really. The good thing was I still lived at home those first couple of years and went to the university where she taught before transferring to Harvard. My mom insisted. And my mom always gets what she wants."

"Oh, you're preaching to the choir on that one," said Katie. "My mom rules the house. Crazy thing is, she's Italian, and we're sort of known for being loud, but she never raises her voice. Just gives you the eye, and she has a gift for the guilt. Every conversation goes the same way with her. Guilt, gossip about the neighbors, guilt, gossip about the family and she finishes off with a good dose of—"

"Guilt," Mac answered for her.

Katie laughed. "Exactly. But I love her. I love them all, but taking the job at Stonegate was the best thing that ever happened to me, even though it's kind of consumed me, too. The day I left, my mother gave me the scariest look. Then she pointed a spatula at me and told me to behave myself."

They pulled up in front of the university. Before getting out of the car she acted like her mother and gave him "the look." She and her brothers had feared that more than their father's disappointment, and that was saying something.

Mac did a fake cringe. "Our mothers need to meet," he joked as he handed her the keys. "I'll see you in a couple of hours?" Mac asked.

"Actually, I'm going to walk you up to the lab and then I'll go."

"Katie, the security guard is right there. You don't have to worry."

She gave him "the look" again.

"Sorry." He quickly held up his hands in surrender.

She smiled warmly. "You're learning," she said.

AN HOUR LATER she met Roland in his office. It was a small glass enclosure, so at least they had some privacy.

"Any more from Caroline?"

He shook his head. "She told her barrister that she didn't have anything more to say and she didn't know anything about another accomplice. Bunch of bollocks, if you ask me."

"She's lying, but she's too selfish to protect someone, so whoever this is he or she must be part of her plan." Katie chewed on the inside of her lips. "How is the sketch going?"

Roland sat down behind his desk. "Right now it looks like half of the white males in London. There are no real distinguishing features."

"Do you have a copy?"

He found one and handed it to her. "I thought you could show it to Professor Douglas. Maybe it will jog his memory."

Katie eyed the sketch. There was something about

the face that seemed familiar. She was good with faces. She had to be when it came to her work.

"I'll take this over to the lab," she said quietly as she gathered up her things.

"Do you recognize him?"

Katie shrugged. "It looks like someone I met a few days ago at the faculty party, but I can't be sure. The eyes are different and the shape of the jaw. I'd like to see what Professor Douglas thinks and then I'll call you."

Just as she arrived at the university the man's identity flashed in her mind. She tried phoning Mac, but he didn't answer.

Nerves on edge, she called Roland and filled him in. "Mac's not answering his phone. It's probably nothing, but—"

"We're on our way."

Katie hung up and ran. Mac might be in trouble. If anything happened to him, she would never forgive herself. She hit the door to the building so hard the guard was up and out of his seat before she'd got to him.

"Are you the only one on duty?"

"Miss?"

"Listen, I need you to lock down the building. The police will be here any minute. Don't let anyone but them in or out. Do you understand?"

"I say, miss. This isn't how we do things—"

"A man's life is in danger. Please!"

The guard frowned, but removed his keys as if to lock the doors.

Katie took the elevator, then sped toward Mac's office, but she paused for a moment when she heard familiar voices coming from a conference room.

The door was ajar; she listened.

"You must understand I would never willingly hurt you," she heard a man say. She recognized the voice, confirming her assumption about the sketch.

"I simply didn't know what to do, and I wasn't thinking clearly." The man was upset, she didn't want to startle him by swinging open the door.

"It's completely logical," Mac said, obviously trying to calm the man. "Phillip, I'm not sure I wouldn't have done the same thing in your shoes."

Phillip. Yes, she was right.

The other man sighed heavily. "The police will never believe me."

"Yes, they will. We'll make sure of it. When they see the letter she had delivered to you, they won't have any trouble putting the pieces together. The woman is insane."

"But she said if I went to the police I'd regret it forever."

"My friend Katie can help us with that. She'll know what to do. She's smart. She'll know exactly what must be done to protect you from that lunatic."

Katie edged the door farther open and saw Phillip sitting at the end of the table with an antique pistol in front of him.

Phillip hadn't noticed her yet, and she was only two feet from the gun.

As she grabbed for the weapon, the man suddenly jerked in a spasm. She and Mac rushed to keep the man from falling out of his chair.

Katie moved the weapon to her waistband and helped Mac lower the convulsing man to the floor.

Phillip's face was ashen and contorted in pain.

Katie pulled her phone from her pocket.

"Ms. McClure, is everything all right?" Roland yelled through the phone. She could tell from his breathing that he was running.

"Mac is fine, but we need an ambulance now. His friend Phillip is having a heart attack."

"We're in the lobby. Medics are with us."

"Phillip, help is here. You're going to be all right?"

The sick man's eyes began to droop.

Katie squeezed his hand in hers. "Phillip, stay with me now. You have to try to stay calm."

"But Mac…"

"Mac is fine, thanks to you. I know what happened." At least, she had some idea. "I don't want you to worry about all of that right now. I want you to focus on taking slow steady breaths. It's important that you—"

"I can't go to jail. I won't…"

His eyes drooped again.

Katie didn't want to make promises she couldn't keep, but she didn't want the man to die. "I don't know all the facts—just what I heard through the door—but it sounds to me like we all know who is at fault and it isn't you, Phillip. Relax. I'm going to help you and so is Mac."

She didn't think it possible, but his skin was even grayer.

"Ms. McClure?" Roland was outside the door.

"We're in here."

The medics rushed in and Katie and Mac backed away. She noticed Mac's hands were shaking slightly, and she couldn't blame him. He'd been through so much.

More than anything she wanted to comfort Mac. How could she care this strongly for a man she'd met only a few days ago?

She didn't know the answer, only that she did.

And the idea of having to leave him was ripping her apart. More than once today she'd thought about quitting her job at Stonegate, but they were still playing catch-up, even with Katie consulting on every case. Her friend Mar needed her, and Katie wouldn't let her down.

Katie also knew there was no way Mac, even if he wanted to, could just up and move back to the States. His research was here.

They were at an impasse, one that left her sad and alone once again.

19

MAC AND KATIE STOOD in silence as they rode the elevator up to her suite. She could have insisted on taking him back to his apartment in Knightsbridge, but she didn't. He took that as a good sign that she wasn't quite ready to say goodbye.

He wasn't.

"I need to make a few calls and let the gang at Stonegate know what happened."

"That's fine," Mac said as they exited the elevator. "If you're hungry, I'll order some food."

"Oh, thanks," she said.

They were being too polite, each unwilling to point out what stood between them.

Katie went straight to her bedroom and shut the door. He could hear her chatting.

He picked up the in-room dining menu and saw something that made him smile. The spa had something he knew she would love. He quickly ordered food and the spa treatment. Katie deserved it after everything she'd done.

She'd been so brave in that room with Phillip. She'd

taken control and treated him with respect, even though she didn't have the whole story at the time.

Phillip had come to the conference room on the pretence of talking to Mac about the research. Then he had pulled the gun out of his jacket and asked Mac to sit down while he explained something. He'd gone on to tell him that he'd received a death threat from Caroline. She'd told him step-by-step what he had to do, from renting the car with cash to running Mac over.

Only, Phillip couldn't do it. He was on his way to tell Mac when he'd been blinded by the sun and accidentally clipped him with the car.

"I panicked," Phillip told him, worry etched on his face. "All those people were watching and I didn't know what to do, so I drove away as fast as I could. Praying you were safe."

Mac believed him. That explained why the car had been at such an odd angle. Phillip had been pulling up to stop and Mac had been right in front of him.

Phillip had confessed the gun he'd brought wasn't even loaded. "Though I wish it were. I'd off myself here and now, and be done with this awful business. She's going to send someone to kill me now. I don't think I can take the waiting."

Thankfully, Phillip had survived the heart attack. Mac had refused to press charges against the man, although there wasn't much he could do about saving his job. The dean refused to see reason.

It was all such a waste.

Katie came out of her bedroom dressed in her exercise clothes.

There was a knock on the door and Mac answered.

"Good evening, sir, we're here with the—" Mac cut him off with his hand.

"Hold on one second. I'm going to take her out on the terrace—you get everything set up."

The man gave him a knowing smile.

"Come on, Katie, we'll enjoy the view from the terrace," Mac instructed.

Pushing his hands away, she tried to look around him as he grabbed their coats. "Mac, it's like thirty degrees outside and snowing. I'm not going out on the terrace."

Mac pulled her coat over shoulders and gently led her to the door. "Come on, it's beautiful outside."

Katie tried to resist, but she let him guide her through the door. Hopping from one foot to the other, she said, "Mac, it really is cold out here."

Mac wrapped his arms around her waist and kissed her for a full minute.

"Okay, yes. That's warmer," she said softly against his lips.

Turning her away from him, he wrapped his coat around her. He squeezed her tight.

It was one of those perfect moments. The lights twinkled like glitter in the night sky.

Katie sighed in his arms.

"It's like a postcard, and if it weren't so dark I would take a picture."

"That's the point. These moments are all ours. No one else can own them."

Her shoulders tensed.

"We could have so many of these moments that we won't know what to do with them," he said, thinking of the future.

Every time she thought about having to leave, he saw the pain in her eyes. He knew it, because he felt the same way.

She twisted so she could see his face. "I don't think we should go there."

"We're going to have a future together, Katie. Whatever is going on between us, it's good. I'm not saying it won't take some work. But we have to try."

"I want to believe you. Part of me wants to let go and allow myself to feel all of this. But I come from a world where there really aren't happy endings."

"That's not true, Katie. Remember what you told me about your job. You said since you made the move to Stonegate that things have been better, and the cases do have happy endings. And you told me that story the other day about your friend Mar who found romance in an unlikely place. They made it—why couldn't we? I want to be with you."

She moved away toward the terrace wall. "We've known each other such a short time. I want you, too—I think we both understand that. But you live here, and my life is in Texas."

"Does that matter so much, really? We're both involved in our work and don't have much time to date. I can manage to come to the States in the interest of research at least once every two months or so. And you said the company has cases in Europe all the time. Maybe you can take some of those on. You can stop by on your way home from wherever you are."

She sighed again. "You have thought about this."

"Haven't you?" Mac gently pulled her chin so he could see her eyes. "Tell me you haven't thought about trying to make this work somehow?"

Katie closed her eyes. "It's useless. I'm sorry. I have to be practical. I can't live in a world of maybes and fairy tales. The real world doesn't work that way, Mac."

"I don't know, Katie. I think happy endings are just like any experiment. You plug in the right variables and you never know, the equation might work."

Mac heard the door shut in the room.

Taking her hand, he led her back inside the suite to the bathroom.

The lights were out, but there were at least thirty candles, and the bath was filled with rose petals.

Expecting her to squeal with delight, he was surprised when he saw her expression.

"Have I mentioned in the last few hours that you don't play fair, Dr. Douglas?" Her face was grim.

"Not when I want something as much as I want you."

With that, she was in his arms.

Mac kissed her with everything he was. He would find a way to make it work. She was his Katie, and she would be until the end of time.

20

KATIE'S HANDS SHOOK so hard, she could barely button her blouse. She finally gave up and grabbed one of the long-sleeved T-shirts from her bag. It would be more comfortable on the plane anyway.

The plane. That ridiculous machine that would take her away from Mac, and there was nothing she could do about it. They'd had a weekend of dreams. Lovely, beautiful and passionate, and everything had come to a screeching halt this morning. He still believed they could have a long-distance relationship, but she knew better.

Katie could barely look at Mac without feeling physically ill from the want of him. She'd been sharp with him, even mean at times, but he only smiled and kissed her.

The calm way he handled everything from room service to helping her find her favorite bra, which they'd lost somewhere under the couch, irritated the hell out of her. Why wasn't he upset? Had he already grown tired of her?

She touched her fingers to her lips. They'd made love

so many times that it took her a moment to remember when they'd even been on the couch to lose that bra.

She stared up at the ceiling of the hotel bedroom. The day had come too soon, but she was a big girl. No regrets. She'd taken the leap and risked everything. For the first time in her life she'd allowed herself to let go and live. And she'd loved every minute of it.

It was worth it.

Keep telling yourself that.

No matter how much pain it caused, this had been the most incredible three days of her life.

No regrets. No regrets. That would be her mantra, every time she felt as though her heart was being ripped from her chest.

Katie knew there were people who had never experienced what she and Mac had shared. He'd been right all along. Their connection was special. And she wouldn't ruin their last minutes together being ungrateful.

"Mac," she said as she pulled her bag back into the bedroom. He wasn't there.

She went to the living room, but he wasn't there, either. She was about to check the other bathroom when she saw movement out on the terrace.

"Hey, is everything okay?"

He turned to her and smiled. That grin washed all her cares away.

"Yes, you look beautiful."

She smirked. No matter how many times he said it, she would never get used to the compliment. "And you're one hot professor."

That made him laugh. "I'm not sure anyone has ever said that to me."

"Trust me, your students—girls and probably some of the guys—are thinking it every day in class."

She glanced at her watch. "I guess I'm ready to go."

"You know you could try detecting on this side of the pond. Your friends would understand."

The thought had crossed her mind. "I wish I could, Mac. But uprooting my life again for some—well, you aren't some guy. We just met and this is all happening so fast. One of us has to be realistic."

He started to speak, but she put a finger to his lips. "I'm not saying we can't try this long-distance thing, but we need to live in the real world."

She grabbed his hand. "Come on. I'll be late to the airport. You know, you don't have to come with me. The university is on the way. The cab can drop you off there. And I'm going straight to security."

"No way. That's an extra hour I get to spend with you in the taxi. You're stuck with me." He picked up her bag.

"Wait." She pulled on his coat lapels, forcing his face to hers.

Then she kissed him, capturing his lips with hers and putting everything she felt about him into that one kiss.

"Oh, Katie," he growled, turning the kiss more passionate.

When she finally pulled away, she forced herself to smile. "There. That way you won't forget me," she said with fake cheerfulness.

Mac watched her carefully. "Never going to happen. Your entire body is imprinted on my brain, from your lips to that sexy purple polish you wear on your toes.

I may forget to pick up my cleaning on Tuesdays, but I have a photographic memory. You have been down-loaded right here." He tapped the side of his head.

She smiled at her dotty old professor

"You really are something."

He tugged her hair.

"That's what you tell me."

THIS WAS TOUGHER than Mac could ever have imagined. He stood with Katie in the passenger-unloading lane at Heathrow. Security was tight, and the officer had already motioned once for them to move along. The taxi driver honked.

"This is for you." He handed Katie a locket. It had a small rose engraved into the platinum. "I know lockets are kind of old-fashioned, but I saw it in a store the other day and it made me think of you. I wanted you to have a reminder that you are always my favorite rose."

She opened it to find one picture she'd taken of him the day at the greenhouse, and one of her that he'd taken on the balcony at the hotel.

"Mac, it's beautiful. Thank you."

"Don't put it on until after you go through security, but then I want you to leave it on. What I'm about to say is corny as hell, but I want to be close to your heart, always." Mac couldn't believe the sappy lovesick words falling out of his lips.

She slapped at his chest. "You're too sweet." She sniffled. "I'm trying to be tough and not turn into one of those weepy girls at the airport, and you go and do something like this."

Mac couldn't help but chuckle. The tough-girl

comment cracked him up. He'd never seen her anything but.

"Stop laughing, jerk." She pushed the tears away with her mitten.

There was never a more beautiful woman than Katie, and he loved her, even when she was mad at him. He kissed her one last time.

"Promise you'll call me when you land?"

"Yes. Thank you." Her voice was hoarse with emotion.

"Okay, miss. I'm sorry, but if you're boarding a flight you'll have to go. We can't tie up the lanes any longer," the officer interrupted, spoiling their last moment. Mac squeezed her hard and handed her the suitcase.

"I'll talk to you when you land."

She nodded and kissed his cheek.

Then she was gone.

The day had arrived long before it should have, and he wasn't handling it well. Sure, he'd tried to be strong for her, but every time he'd looked at her that morning his chest had tightened to the point where he couldn't breathe.

Mac jumped back into the cab and gave the driver the address for the university.

The driver seemed to sense he wasn't in the mood to talk, and for that he was grateful. Mac watched the city pass by and every mile they drove away from the airport created a giant space between him and Katie.

Mac pulled out his phone and went through the pictures he'd taken of her. The photos of her laughing hard were his absolute favorites. The joy in her eyes was enough to sustain him, at least for a few weeks until he could find a way to see her again.

Katie didn't believe they could make a long-distance relationship work, but Mac had hope. He was a stupid lovesick fool. Of that he was certain, but if they didn't try he knew they would both have regrets.

Maybe he was the one who needed to make a serious life change, one that could alter the course he'd so carefully planned for himself.

Yes, he was well and fully enraptured with this woman who had butted her way into his life, and he'd be damned if he'd let her go without a fight.

21

As Katie's plane landed at JFK she stared up at the luggage bays on the plane. She could grab a flight to Austin right away, or she could take a later one and visit her family. As much as they drove her crazy, she could use a good distraction.

Unable to stand hearing his voice quite yet, she sent him a quick text. Made it to NY, phone's on fritz again. Hope you get this. K.

Coward.

Yes, but right now it's about surviving the next few days.

Without thinking much, she found herself on the subway with her bags, heading to her old neighborhood. Preoccupied with thoughts of Mac, she didn't realize she'd arrived at her destination until she saw the McClure's Pub sign in front of her. The pub was in the corner of an eight-story building. Katie's family owned the building and occupied the top two floors. The rest were small studio apartments they rented.

She watched through the windows for a moment. GJ was behind the bar telling one of his stories to an audience on bar stools. There was a crowd behind them, all listening, and then the whole place broke out in laughter.

Tears brimmed in her eyes. She missed this part of home. Her brother Liam smiled as he wiped off the tables. He'd probably heard the story at least a few hundred times. GJ had a gift for making the same tales always sound new, and she never grew tired of them.

The whole family, including her two brothers, pitched in around the pub. It was nearing six, and she knew her mother would be in the kitchen fixing an array of hot dishes and sandwiches to be served along with the beer and whiskey.

Katie sniffed her tears away and put her hand on the door.

The smell of stale beer and beef stew assailed her. *Home.*

She swallowed the small lump in her throat and rolled her bags through the crowd. GJ had turned on ESPN, where they were gearing up for a Rangers hockey game. The Bronx loved its hockey.

GJ was busy pouring beer as Katie shoved her bags into a corner behind the bar. When he turned, he saw her and let out a whoop.

"It's my girl," he yelled, then embraced her in a welcoming hug.

"I missed you." She squeezed him hard.

He lifted her chin with his hand. "What's wrong? Your eyes are sad." Yes, the man was observant.

She smiled. "I'm fine, I promise. Had a long flight from London. The jet lag kills me."

His eyebrows rose. "Now, you won't be telling tales to me, lass. Your heart's been broken—it's written on your face plain as day. I'll hear the truth from you soon enough." Without taking his eyes off her, he yelled, "Liam, come give your sister a hug, and then take over the bar."

Her brother, who had been cleaning the tables, ran to greet her. Well, as much as he could through the crowd. He picked her up in his arms and swung her around. "Peanut, you're home!" He laughed as he twirled her around.

"Put me down, you big ape! And stop calling me peanut." He set her down carefully. It was useless to tell him to stop calling her by the name he'd given her when she was born. Liam swore she looked like a shriveled-up peanut as an infant.

"Why didn't you tell us you were coming home? Does Mom know?"

"I most certainly did not." Her mother stood in the doorway to the kitchen, wiping her hands on her apron. Katie walked into the arms open wide for her. Her mother smelled of roses and lasagna, the mixture one of Katie's favorite scents. It meant she was home.

She squeezed her mother, and then did it again for good measure. Her mom backed away and took Katie's face in her hands. "Oh, my. It's a man. Let's talk. Into the kitchen with you." She shooed Katie in. "You men tend the bar. I want to talk to my daughter alone," she announced, closing the door behind her.

The pub kitchen was where Katie had spent a good portion of her life. Stainless steel appliances lined the walls. The big freezer door was at the back of the room, and a long stainless steel prep table was in the middle with several stools around it.

Katie sat on one of the stools while her mother poured

two cups of coffee and magically came up with a plate of Katie's favorite chocolate chip cookies.

"Tell me about him," her mother insisted as she pulled up a stool next to Katie. "All of it."

Katie thought about how much to tell, but once she began, she couldn't stop. The words poured out of her like a heavy rain. She expected her mother to admonish her for falling for a client.

"Katie, love, you care about him, so you need to find a way to make it work." Her mother rose and began peeling potatoes. "I read stories all the time about people who have successful long-distance relationships. It isn't easy, but if you care enough you make it work."

"That's what Mac says." She sighed. "It hurts so much right now. How will I feel in a week? Even if we talk every day—I just don't know that it wouldn't be better to make a clean break. I'm not sure I can live apart from him like this. I mean, I've known him less than two weeks, but…"

But what? She remembered what Mar had gone through when Jackson was taken in by the CIA. For more than two months Mar had no idea if she'd ever see him alive again. In the end it had worked out. They had a romance Katie had seen only in romantic movies, but it hadn't come without some heartache.

"That's something only you can decide, Katie. All that talk about love being easy when the right people find each other is nonsense.

"Love is hard," her mother continued. "You have to work at relationships every day. If you are serious about him, then you fight for him. You're a strong woman— you always have been. I've never seen you lie down and accept defeat. That isn't who you are, Katie. You're a fighter. Every good thing you have in your life has taken work, and it's always worth it. A little distance is all you're worried about? There are worse things. You two can call, and Daniel told me they have those video chat things on the computers so you can see each other. If it's meant to be, you'll find a way to be with him no matter what."

Her mother had a point. Katie had set herself up as some kind of victim, but the truth was Mac was in the same boat. He wanted to fight for them. If she did the same, then they could fight together, and two were always better than one.

That might be the corniest thing she'd thought in a long time, but it was true. No one had ever made her feel the way Mac did, and she wasn't ready to let go. No matter how much she tried to convince herself that she could.

"The way I see it, love's a commodity we can't afford to waste. My relationship with your father isn't always easy." That was no joke. They'd spent a good portion of Katie's life nagging one another. She'd even seen her mother throw a pot at her father, but they always made up. She'd seen the way they looked at each other, and that's how she knew that kind of love was possible.

"You're right, Mom. I guess I have some thinking to do." *I'm going to fight.* She'd try her best to solve the long-distance problem, and even if it didn't work out in the end, Mac was worth whatever pain she might go through.

A man cleared his throat behind her and she turned to find her father there. She jumped up and threw her arms around him. "Pops, how are you?"

"I'm fine, peanut. You look tired."

"Just back from London, and I can't sleep on planes. I missed you."

"We missed you, too, lass. Now, what's this I hear about man troubles?"

Katie scrunched her face. The last thing she wanted to do was discuss her love life with her father.

"Katie met a young man in London, and she's fallen hard. Sounds like he has, too. She's trying to decide what to do about dating long distance."

Her dad rubbed the top of her head as he had when she was a child. "You fight. That's what we McClures do. If we want something we go after it, and we don't let obstacles stand in our way. You're made of sterner stuff. Now, buck up and be smart about it."

Leave it to her dad to say it straight.

She chuckled. "Dad, you were never one to mince words."

"Mom—" Daniel came down the stairs "—what's for dinner? Holy hell, Katie's here," he said as he made his way into the kitchen.

"You watch your mouth in my home, young man, or I'll wash it out with soap." Her mom wasn't kidding.

Katie had cussed like crazy on the job when she worked as a cop, but at home she'd catch herself and had come up with some pretty crazy words, from *fudge knuckles* to *shisterman,* to avoid her mother's wrath.

There were more hugs, and then they all settled around the steel table.

GJ walked in, with Liam right behind him.

"Who's tending bar?" her father asked.

"Carly's here. Happy hour crowd has thinned. She'll be okay for a while, until the regulars come in."

At the mention of Carly's name she noticed Daniel's head pop up.

"I can go out and help her," he offered.

"Not until you've had your dinner," their mother said. "Like Grandpa Joe says, Carly can handle it for now. I haven't had my family together for almost a year."

It was more like six months, but Katie wasn't about to argue with her.

"We're going to sit down together," her mother said as she dished up lasagna. Katie noticed that her dad's plateful was out of a different casserole dish.

"Why can't I have the real thing?" her father protested.

"Because you aren't kickin' off and leaving me with this bunch to handle on my own." Her mother waved a spatula around. "You're going to eat healthy if I have to stuff it down your throat."

Her father mumbled under his breath, but she noticed the grin as he bent his head to say the blessing.

Once grace was said, the table erupted in conversations as everyone spoke at once. It was the McClure way. Katie missed all of it—but not so much that she wanted to move home. The separation from her family was good for her, but she did miss these big loud meals.

Katie sighed happily as she glanced around the table. She wanted this some day. She wanted it for her and Mac. A large happy family.

What was she thinking? A month ago she hadn't been sure she even wanted children. Now she was planning them with a man who lived six thousand miles away.

"So is this man you have your heart set on British?" GJ asked.

"Katie has a boyfriend?" her brothers questioned in unison.

She chuckled. Nothing had changed. "I wouldn't call him that exactly. He's a man I'm interested in. And, GJ, he was born in California, and he's a professor working at a university in London. I can't talk about his research, but his work is important. The kind of stuff that could change the fate of countries."

"Oh, Katie likes an egghead," Liam scoffed.

Katie punched his arm and was gratified by the wince he gave her. "Listen, you guys would like him. Yes, he's smart, but he's not at all what you would think a professor would be like. He's gorgeous, funny and—"

Daniel made gagging sounds.

Everyone laughed.

"Whatever." Katie chuckled. "You know, I thought talking about him would hurt, but I really feel better. Thanks, Mom."

"Katie, love, that's why we're here," her mother said as she filled Pops's coffee cup without even looking.

Daniel was the first one finished. He took his dishes to the industrial washer and was out the door and into the pub before his mother could say a word.

He'd always had a crush on Carly, but he'd never acted on it. Carly had been working at the pub the past year and a half as a bartender and waitress. She was going to graduate school for a master's and later a doctoral degree in psychology. She liked the bar atmosphere because it was a microcosm of humanity.

"Let me guess," Katie said, "Danny still hasn't asked Carly out?"

Liam laughed. "Not even close. He can barely speak

when she's around. Funniest thing I've ever seen. Big bad Daniel rendered speechless by a girl."

That earned him a swat with the dish towel. "You leave your brother alone, and I don't want you talking trash about him when she's around. I heard you the other day. I'll have none of that," her mother warned.

Liam grimaced. "I was just trying to break the ice for him," he said.

He received another swat.

"Ma." He jumped up and took his dishes to the washer. "I'm going to call the police if you don't stop that abuse." He put his arms around his mom's neck and kissed her cheek. "Wait, I am the police. I've got duty in an hour. Will you be here when I get back?" he asked Katie.

She shook her head. "Nah, I'm catching the red-eye out tonight. I've got to report back to work tomorrow morning. We have a couple of big cases coming up that they need me to consult on."

The messages from Mar had been on her voice mail when Katie had checked them before the plane took off. Her friend hadn't minded her taking a few days to see London. Mar had wanted her to take her time and not worry about the office. But when Katie had checked her email at the agency, she knew Mar was only being nice about giving her time off. That was one of the reasons she couldn't leave her friend, she was too nice. They had a backlog of cases and Katie was needed more than ever.

"Hmm, la-di-da, peanut's a fancy consultant. High-flying corporate girl." Liam walked around the table and gave her a hug. "Don't stay away so long the next time," he whispered as he rubbed a noogie into her head. "And whoever the guy is, he's a lucky one."

Katie swallowed the lump in her throat and hugged him back.

Liam was wrong. She was the lucky one. Being with her family had reminded her of what was most important. More than anything she wanted to be with Mac. She would do whatever it took to make that happen, even if it meant quitting her job.

22

AT THE OFFICE the next afternoon, Katie could barely keep her eyes open. After four cups of coffee and two meetings, she was beat. She'd gone straight from the airport to the office. Other than the twenty minutes she'd spent freshening up and changing clothes in her private bathroom, she'd been working nonstop.

"Thank you for consulting on those cases," Mar said as she walked into Katie's office. "You are always so good at seeing these situations from an objective viewpoint. I hadn't even thought about bringing in Jackson on the Bryer case, but you're right. His security skills would come in handy. That is, if I can get him away from the CIA. I thought when he left that place he'd be done, but so far he's spent more time consulting there than here."

Katie's office was next to Mar's, and they were even decorated in the same art deco style, as the women shared similar tastes.

"So, are you going to tell me about it?"

Katie jolted. "What?"

"The man, whoever he is. You met someone while you were on the case there, didn't you?"

Mar's profiling abilities had really improved. Pretty soon no one would be able to keep a secret around the office.

Did she wear her emotions that easily? Katie had always thought she was good at hiding things. She wouldn't lie to her friend, but she also didn't feel like discussing Mac quite yet. She needed to talk to him about some things. Find out where they really stood. To be honest, she wanted to find out if he missed her as much as she did him just twenty-four hours after they'd parted.

"I was busy with the case—you know that."

Mar nodded. "It's okay if you don't want to talk about it. I've been there." She smiled at Katie with so much understanding that it almost made her cry.

Katie sighed. "When I do want to talk, I promise you are the first ear in line."

Mar tucked a file folder under her arm. "Any time. Now, why don't you go home and get some rest. I can tell the jet lag is killing you. Take tomorrow off—you've earned it."

"No, that's not necessary. I just need a good night's rest tonight. I feel like I've missed too much work already. The longer I'm gone, the bigger the backlog."

"Go home. That's an order," she said with a wink.

Katie didn't need to be told twice. She grabbed her bags and zipped out the door.

Her condo was a two-bedroom loft with fantastic views of downtown Austin and a great kitchen, so Katie had no complaints. But it never really felt like home. It was the place where she slept and sometimes watched television. It was already furnished, so the only things that belonged to Katie were her clothes, a few pictures of her family and the electronics.

There was also a fully loaded gym downstairs, but she was too tired to work out.

It was nearly five, so Katie had stopped to pick up a chicken salad from the French bakery and a chocolate croissant she couldn't resist. After placing the food on the wooden dining table, she flipped on the television. But she couldn't stand the idea of eating alone.

Picking up her phone she dialed.

"Katie?"

Mac's voice made her hands shake. "I miss you," she said over the lump in her throat.

"I miss you, too. Did you get my messages? I thought you were going to call me when you landed." He sounded worried and she felt guilty.

"I'm sorry. I—I was upset and stopped to see my family. I just wasn't thinking. And I'm sorry for being a coward and sending you a text. I promise it was only because I didn't want to break down like a total wimp."

"Katie, you're never a wimp. How's your dad doing?"

Leave it to Mac to be so thoughtful.

"He's good. Mom is taking great care of him whether he wants her to or not. I'm really sorry I'm calling you so late."

Mac chuckled and the sound calmed her.

There was a long pause.

"I told you to call me any time of day and I meant it. Katie, tell me what's wrong." The man was so perceptive, and always seemed to know what was going on in her head.

"It's tougher than I thought it would be," she said. "I hurt, Mac."

There was another long pause. "I know, trust me. I haven't been able to think about anything but you since you left. But we can do this. We'll make it work."

She sighed. "Thank you. I needed to hear you say that. I wasn't sure at first. I thought it would be easier to make a clean break, but I can't do it. We have to try, Mac. What we have is—"

"Amazing and special and we aren't going to throw it away. I don't want you to give up, baby. We will find a way."

"Mac, I want to fight for this, but I need to know…" She couldn't quite get the words out.

"Katie, never doubt how much I care about you. I'm ready to chuck all my research so I can be with you. If there weren't so many people depending on me, I'd be on the first plane out of here. But I have to get through this critical point. There's too much riding on this next stage. But I can't stand being away from you, baby. It's the toughest thing I've ever had to do."

A tear slid down her cheek and she took a deep shuddering breath.

"Oh, Katie, don't cry." His voice was hoarse with emotion.

"I don't cry." She shoved the offensive water from her face. Well, she hadn't cried until she met Mac. He'd opened her heart, and now she felt everything.

"Besides, if I did cry it would be a happy tear." She cleared her throat. "I just needed to know you wanted me as much as I do you." She shoved her food away. "Mac, I need you so badly right now." Her body still craved his touch. That was the toughest part of this.

There was a choked sound as Mac coughed on the other end of the phone line. "Turn your computer on, Katie."

This time it was she who was surprised. "Mac?"

"Do it, Katie. That's an order."

She smiled as she picked up the computer. "You know I don't take orders very well," she said huskily.

"You will tonight, baby. I'm going to make love to you."

Katie couldn't believe how he could do that over the computer, but agreed to play his game. She needed him, even this way. As she moved to the bedroom her body heated from her head to her toes, and her panties were already damp.

"Put the computer where I can see, and undress for me," Mac told her.

"Mac." Katie looked up the ceiling. Now it was all a little too real. She felt silly, but positioned the laptop so the camera was on her. She adjusted the volume and disconnected their phone call.

"Katie—" his voice was husky again "—I need to see you. All of you."

She shook her head. "I'll do it if you do."

"I promise," he said, "but you first."

Katie tilted the computer screen so he could see her. Taking a deep breath, she undid the buttons of her blouse. She slipped it off her shoulders and stood there in her bra and jeans.

"All of it, baby."

This time she smiled. "I took off my shirt. You take off your pants and underwear. I want to see your cock."

Mac laughed. "Well, thanks to what you just said I'm hard as a rock now."

Katie's insecurities about their long-distance relationship fled with her newfound power. Her words could make him hard.

"I want you to hold your cock while I strip, Mac."

"Katie, if you keep talking like that I'm going to come before we ever get started."

She laughed.

Soon he was devoid of his pants, his huge cock waving like a stiff flag in front of her. "I wish I could taste you. Slide my tongue down that huge shaft and—"

"Stop it." Mac ordered, then bent down so she could see his smile. "Strip for me. No more talking." He winked at her to take the fire from his gruff words.

She gave him a little salute and attacked the clasp of her bra. Her nipples bounced up, perky with need. She imagined Mac's hands on her. Eyes closed, she moved her hands to her breasts, pinching the nipples the way he had.

"Katie, I'm going to explode right here and now. You look so hot. Your mouth. Your nipples. I want to taste you. Take off your pants. I want to see if you're wet for me."

Katie's hands shook slightly as she slipped off her jeans. Had she ever needed a man so much in her life?

No. The answer was simple. Mac was it for her. She took the panties down with the jeans and stood before him completely naked.

"Have I told you how beautiful you are?"

Every time he said that, her heart plunged to her toes and back up again.

"Now put the computer to your left on the bed so I can watch you, and then lie down."

"Watch me what?" She did as he asked.

"Look at me, Katie." She did and she saw his cock in his hand so hard and ready for her. A drop of cum leaked out.

"Rub that with your thumb," she said. "Pretend it's me. I want to taste you so badly, it hurts right now."

This time Mac did what she said, groaning slightly with the action. "I want to be inside you," he said.

"Me, too. I want you pounding me senseless. I need it."

"Touch yourself, baby. Slide your fingers into that hot pink flesh and rub that nub like I would if I were there." His voice was husky with need and his words made her entire body shake.

Katie's fingers slid down to do what he asked. The second she touched herself she gasped. Her body was so tightly wound it begged for release. She no longer cared he was watching, or that they were thousands of miles apart. Her fingers slipped in and out of her body, alternately rubbing the nub and sliding a finger into her pink folds. She thought of his fingers, the way he touched her that stoked a fire so deep, she burned with desire.

Her eyes closed and her breathing quickened.

She heard a moan and realized it was her.

Her back arched and she whispered, "Mac." Turning so she could see him, she gasped.

"I know, Katie. I know." The look in his eyes told her he felt the same way. She watched as his hand slid up and down his cock. The sight tightened her lower belly and she felt the moisture in her folds increase. She had never thought watching a man pleasuring himself could be so hot.

Mac pumped his cock faster and faster and she imagined it inside her. Pounding her senseless.

"Pinch your nipple with your other hand, Katie. It's my teeth and tongue sliding around, sucking."

Her hand slid to her breast while her other one continued to rub faster and faster. "Mac," she gasped as she pinched. Her body shook with an orgasm so strong he saw stars for a minute.

"That's right. Keep going," he encouraged.

She opened her eyes to see him moving his hand even faster, his look so intent on her that she knew he was thinking of his cock deep inside her.

Katie wanted to stop and watch him, but she didn't. She stayed right with him, her hands keeping time with his. "I want to be sucking you right now," she whispered. "Your cock hitting the back of my throat, to feel you exploding in my mouth. Let me taste you now, Mac. Come for me," she cried on the verge of another orgasm.

Katie's back arched as the sensations poured through her body, and she watched as Mac's seed poured from his body onto the towel he'd laid on his thighs.

Her body shuddered and his did the same. Watching him this way was every bit as hot as being there with him. Okay, maybe not as good, but close enough. They'd enjoyed each other and the miles apart didn't matter a bit.

Mac opened his eyes and smiled at her. "That was amazing," he whispered.

She nodded, not trusting her voice yet.

"I miss you." His smile was still there, but she saw the sadness in his eyes.

She shoved a tiny tear away with the back of her hand.

"Are you crying? Don't—this is good. We can survive this. It'll be tough for a little while, but like your mom said, it's meant to be, so we'll find a way."

She cleared her throat and sat up. Grabbing her shirt, she wrapped it around her. "I told you I don't cry," she said. "I was overcome with the orgasm. That's all."

"Oh, yeah. That's right. You're my tough girl. So what are you doing tomorrow night about this time?"

That made her laugh out loud.

The laughter helped expel some of the tension she felt and she was grateful for his wonderful sense of humor. It was one of many things she adored about him. This was definitely worth fighting for, and as her dad had said, Katie was a fighter. She'd never back down from a challenge, and that was exactly what this was. It was up to Katie to find an answer.

She smiled at her man.

"I think I have a date with you."

23

Two weeks later

KATIE TOOK A DEEP BREATH as she stepped through
Stonegate's doors. The meeting with her colleagues was
in an hour and she prayed she had everything in order.
Mac hadn't helped, what with him being a frequent distraction, but in a good way.

They'd agreed to leave their webcams on when they
were home. He'd even left his on when he was in the
lab. A few times a day she'd click on the window and
watch him work. He'd smile almost as if he knew she
was watching, but he wouldn't say anything. It was as
if she was a voyeur, and she had to admit she kind of
liked it. She'd grown quite comfortable with their video
sex chats, too. Mac, always the creative one, had come
up with some amazing ideas.

There were also the flowers. Every day he sent her a
dozen roses. Her condo was full of them, and she was
running out of space. But each time she walked in her
front door she was assailed by the smell and it sent her
straight to the computer to chat with Mac.

However, nothing substituted for the real thing. Katie unlocked her office and walked in. She had some time before the rest of the gang showed up, but she needed it to get herself settled. She'd never done anything like this proposal. The past few years had been about solving other people's problems. They'd bring her a case and she would take care of it.

This time she was the one with a problem. It was insane what she wanted to do, but she had to try. For her, there were no other options. Katie pulled open her laptop and checked her figures again. She'd also done a couple of maps to show specific areas where they had cases around the world. All of this would prove why opening a branch of the agency in Europe was a necessity.

It wasn't long before people straggled into the office. Mar stopped by to say good-morning.

"You've been working so hard I thought maybe you could use this," she said as she set down a cup of coffee with a chocolate doughnut.

Katie didn't know if her nerves could stomach the chocolate heaven sitting on her desk, but the coffee was appreciated. "Thank you. I have to admit I'm a bit nervous today."

Mar sat down in the chair across from her. "I've known you for a very long time, and I've never seen you nervous. Tell me what this special project is about. Maybe I can help."

Several times in the past week Katie had wanted to share her thoughts with her friend, to get Mar's opinion on some key points, but first she'd had to make sure she had all her facts straight. Still, she didn't know how the others would take her news, and it would help if she had Mar on her side.

"Do you have time before the meeting for me to explain it to you?" Katie asked.

Mar crossed her legs. "Katie, I always have time for you. Tell me."

Katie brought up the video presentation she'd put together on her computer and turned the laptop toward Mar. Moving to the other side of the desk, she hit Play.

"I think it's time we opened a branch of Stonegate in Europe." Katie began her presentation.

"We've had more than twenty-seven cases we've closed in London, France, Ireland, Scotland and Italy in the last six months. It takes an enormous amount of travel time to cross the Atlantic and, as you know, the first few days on a case are critical. Having someone on the ground who can be at these locations within a few hours would make a huge difference in the time it takes us to complete our investigations. Beyond those two points, it depletes our human resources here. We're taking valuable time away from the cases we have on this continent by sending key personnel to other countries."

Mar leaned forward and Katie knew she saw the logic. She'd counted on that.

"I'd like to open a branch of the agency in London," Katie concluded.

Mar's eye's opened in surprise and her hand flew to her chest. "You? Really? Katie, why would you want to leave? I know it's been an adjustment for you moving from New York to here, but I thought you were happy."

"Wait, Katie's leaving—what's going on?" That was Chi, the lawyer of the bunch. "You guys," she said to Makala and Patience, who were walking behind Chi, "Mar says Katie's leaving the agency."

There were audible gasps and soon all of Katie's friends were in her office staring at her with surprise.

Moving to the other side of her desk, Katie waved her arms in front of her. "Hold on, people. This isn't what you think. I was only running my proposal by Mar."

She held up a hand in a stop motion to keep them from all speaking at once. "For the record, I love it here. Working with you guys has been the best experience of my life. I mean that. I just had this idea when I was working the case in London, and I wanted to run it by you."

Mar motioned for them all to come forward and watch the presentation on the laptop.

"It makes a lot of sense," Chi said when it was over. "I'm all for anything that cuts down on our traveling overseas. I logged twenty days out of last month, but the preliminaries of the investigation could have been handled by someone else."

"I agree," Mar chimed in. "I think it's a fantastic idea to open a new branch in London. My question, when you walked by, was why Katie would uproot herself again to do it."

Katie looked to the ceiling for answers. There were none there. These were her business associates, but they were also her friends. She chewed on her lip for a few seconds.

"Oh, hell. It's a man," Makala blurted. "Look at her twisting fingers, and I've noticed her flushed cheeks the last week. I thought she was coming down with something, but she's in love."

"Wait a minute." Katie pointed a finger. "No one said anything about love."

There was another collective gasp, and she realized she'd already said too much.

She'd thought about telling them that the move was a way for her to make a real break from her crazy family, but that seemed senseless now.

She cleared her throat. "Yes, I'm interested in someone who lives there. I'm curious about this connection we have and I want to see it through. He's American, but he can't come here right now, as his job won't allow it. So I thought maybe I could set up shop there."

Patience and Makala sat down on the sofa against the wall and Chi took the other chair.

"I have to play devil's advocate here and ask what will happen if things don't work out with him?" Makala never shied away from asking the tough questions.

Katie shrugged. "I'm not moving there only for the man. I actually love London. Honestly. It's a place where I could see myself living the rest of my life, no matter what happens with—" She'd almost said Mac's name. "The man I'm seeing."

"You can't have known him very long," Mar interjected. "You were there for a little over a week."

Laughing, Katie pointed at Mar's huge diamond engagement ring. Jackson had proposed during a trip to Baja last month, and Mar had accepted. They had the kind of relationship Katie hadn't ever thought would be possible for her, but now she wanted that with Mac. "And a few months ago when you met Jackson, did you want to see where that relationship led?"

Mar laughed with her. "True. Very true. I assume your man isn't locked up in some CIA jail. I have to tell you it's not the easiest way to start a relationship."

"No, he's not. Thankfully he has nothing to do with the CIA, or our business for that matter. We honestly couldn't be more different in that respect. But like I said, he can't move here because of his job, and…" Katie paused. "I know it sounds crazy, but I will regret it for the rest of my life if I don't at least try to see it through with him.

"But I'm being honest about opening the new branch, too. I don't know how Chi's been doing it all this time, with the back and forth travel. And what she says is right—we need someone on the ground who can get to our clients in those critical moments. If you guys don't approve of me as the one to do this, then we need to find someone."

For now she left out the part that she'd leave the agency one way or the other. She didn't want to give them an ultimatum. While she was doing what was right for her relationship with Mac, this was a good move for the agency.

Mar stood. She turned toward the other women in the room. "I think Katie is the perfect candidate to do this," she said. "She knows every aspect of this business—the way we work with our clients, the actual casework, and she was the one who helped set up all the new billing procedures when I first took over. She'll need an office, living space and equipment. And we'll need at least one assistant, maybe two to help with the paperwork. Chi, I think you should look into finding a lawyer in London we can work with, too. I had no idea you'd been gone so much. I mean, it seems like you're never here, but twenty days? That's insane with your workload."

"I have some friends who could help with preliminaries and sit second chair if we go to court," Chi said. "I agree. It's a great idea. I think it would take a lot of pressure off many of us. And she'll have access to all of our equipment here."

"Makala and Patience, can you guys check into setting up a lab over there? Our kind of lab, and we'll need to staff it with the right sort of people to run it. You guys could oversee it from here and consult on any of Katie's cases."

"Got it," Makala said, picking up her phone, "but when you're looking for office space, make sure we have plenty of room for the lab. I'll get you the minimum on the dimensions in a bit."

Patience, the SIA forensic archaeologist, rubbed her hands together. "Some of the best FAs in the world live in England."

"You're the best in the world," Katie interrupted her, but she was grateful for her excitement.

"Well, that is sort of true." She smiled. It wasn't a lie. People all over the world came to Patience for help. She had been regarded as number one in her field for the past five years. "But these guys are almost on the same level. This could be really good for us," she said.

Mar put a hand on Katie's shoulder as a show of support. "I'm going to vote yes. So what do you say?"

There was a resounding yes all around.

"Well," said Chi, "I have one stipulation. I want a second bedroom in whatever flat we have for the agency. I'm so tired of staying in hotels and eating out. I'd like to be able to fix my own food."

Katie felt as though all the wind had been let out of her sails. She'd been so ready to fight harder, and they were handing it to her on a silver platter.

"I can't believe you won't be around here." Makala gave her a sad smile.

"I'm going to miss you all, too. And I'll be back here every few months. I have ongoing cases here, too."

Mar hugged her. "So when are we going to hear about this guy? We'd planned two hours for this presentation. I say we put it on hold and go to lunch, get the juicy details."

"I'm in on that," Chi said.

"Me, too," quipped Patience.

"And I'm getting a Bloody Mary." Chi laughed. "Been a long week."

"I hear ya, sister," Mar said. "Jackson's been consulting with the CIA, and I can't wait for him to get home. The days drag by when he's away."

"You are so whipped," Chi teased. "Pining after a man. I didn't think I'd ever see the day. And you—" she pointed to Katie. "I'm not drinking the water around here anymore."

Mar gently punched Chi in the arm. "I can't wait till it happens to you. I live for that moment."

"Never going to happen," Chi responded. "I've sworn off men. I told you that."

Mar snorted. "Yeah, right. We'll see about that. Besides, if Katie can move to London for a man, anything can happen."

"Hey." Katie laughed. "That's so—well, you do have a point. I can't believe I'm doing it, either. But as we always say around here, what's life without a little risk?"

AT THE RESTAURANT across the street from their office, the five women raised their glasses.

"To Katie's new life," Mar toasted her. "May it be better than she ever dreamed."

They clinked glasses.

Katie was hit by all the emotion. She would miss these women. The past year they'd become such a big part of her life. They were always there for one another. It was like a big family, without the zany dysfunction.

"Oh, what's wrong?" Mar asked. "You suddenly look so sad. This should be a happy time for you."

Katie cleared her throat. "Trust me, it is, but it just hit me what a big part of my life you've become."

"Don't be an idiot," Makala said in her direct way. "We aren't going anywhere. And you'll be videoed into the meetings every week. And I have a feeling each of us will be finding a way to visit you in the next six months or so. Now, we are curious about this man of yours...."

"Okay, okay. I'll tell you about him. Well, we met in a bar."

Mar clapped her hands. "That was how Jackson and I began—it's a very lucky start."

Katie smiled, nodded at her friend and continued with her story. She left out the sexy parts, but talked about how after the case they'd realized they had strong feelings for one another. She was worried that her professionalism might be called into question, but honestly, that was when the relationship had become serious. Thankfully, none of them seemed to care.

"Hmm," Makala said.

"Are you going to psychoanalyze me?" Katie asked worriedly.

"Girl, I say if you find someone to love in this world and they love you back, it's all good," Makala interjected.

Katie shook her head. "No, I *like* him—a lot. That's it. Maybe some day we'll have that kind of relationship. Right now it's about seeing if we can have something ongoing. Two weeks after I move there, he may be done with me for all I know." That last bit had been difficult to say.

Was she an idiot? Moving so far away for a relationship with a man?

Yes, she was certifiably insane. Makala was right to question her.

Panic rose in her belly, and she sipped her drink a little faster, praying the alcohol would calm her nerves.

"Hey." Mar patted her arm. "Take a deep breath. You're going to check things out and get us started up over there. No one says it has to be anything but temporary. Don't freak out."

"Oh, I know." Katie pretended to be much braver than she felt. "I was just thinking about everything I need to do before I leave. And I'm excited about the challenge of taking us global, but I'm also worried about the myriad details it'll take to get things up and running." That was true. Her life would once again be about this job, but this time she hoped Mac could help her keep some kind of balance.

"I'm checking your caseload right now," Patience said, looking at her phone. "From what I can see, there's no reason you can't leave right away." She punched a few buttons on her phone. "I've scheduled you for tomorrow noon. You'll have to fly to Dallas, but then it's a straight shot to London."

Katie stared at her, dumbfounded. Tomorrow? She hadn't even had time to talk about the move with Mac. Could she show up on his doorstep like that? Talk about throwing the poor guy for a loop.

"Oh, and if it makes you feel any better, we can put you to work right away. Chi has a witness who has to sign a deposition, and there's a man she was supposed to meet with next week about an Interpol case."

Chi snapped her fingers. "That's right. He's in Rome, and he refused to travel here. Katie, you'd be perfect for the job. The other one is getting a simple signature, which will take you no time at all."

She was going for work. Not just a man. She had to admit this made her feel better. She wouldn't blame Mac if he completely freaked. But it was what she wanted. She'd promised she would do whatever it took, and that meant taking a huge risk on her part.

"Okay, then. London, here I come."

24

THE CLOSER SHE GOT to Mac's flat, the more Katie's nerves increased. So much so that she had to keep breathing deeply to keep the nausea at bay.

What if he thinks I'm crazy for moving here? I should have talked to him about it. I'm going to look like a fool if he's changed his mind about how he feels.

Mac had never given her any reason to doubt he cared for her, but this was a big step.

She'd texted him and told him she was traveling for a case, and that she'd be out of pocket for several hours. Stepping onto the elevator, she had a hard time willing herself to push the button for the penthouse level.

Somehow she'd never managed to visit his apartment. They'd spent most of their time at her hotel. She smiled to herself. Those were some glorious days. The memories gave her the courage she needed to finally push the button.

When the doors opened Mac stood there with a suitcase, and a woman next to him. The breath left Katie and her eyes brimmed with tears.

"Katie." Mac stepped back in shock. "What are you

doing here?" He yanked her off the elevator and into his arms.

He squeezed so tight she couldn't answer.

Pulling away, he put his hand on her cheek and then kissed her, long and hard. For a second she wondered what the other woman must think, but she soon lost herself in Mac.

When he lifted his head, he touched her face again. "I can't believe you're here. Why didn't you tell me?"

Katie wasn't sure what to say. She glanced at the woman and back at him. "I thought it would be a fun surprise."

He chuckled. "It's a good thing you arrived when you did. This is Kerry—she's married to my friend Peter at the university." Katie remembered meeting Peter at the party, but his wife hadn't been with him that evening. If Katie remembered correctly the woman was a pediatric surgeon.

Married. So why was she here?

"I'd just given Kerry the key to the flat so she could take care of my plants while I was gone."

Katie's heart fluttered.

"It's nice to meet you," Kerry said as she held out a hand.

Mac's arms were still wrapped around her, but she wiggled a hand free. "Hi," Katie said. Then she looked back at Mac.

"Where are you going?" she asked him.

"To see you," he said as he squeezed her again. "I finished my paper, and school's finished next week, so I told the dean I needed a break. I gave my students the mid-term exam today, and planned to grade them while you were at work. I've taken a week off to spend with you in the States during the holidays."

That made her giggle. He'd been coming to see her. Relief flowed through her body.

"I believe I'll go, since it looks as though you won't be needing that ride to the airport after all," Kerry said as she handed Mac his keys. "You two enjoy yourselves, and Mac, you bring her to dinner later in the week. That is if you'll be in town then?" she said to Katie.

Katie nodded.

"Thanks, Kerry." Mac picked up his suitcase and while still holding Katie pulled her to his apartment door.

Inside he set the bag down and took her in his arms again. "I've been wanting to do this for weeks." He hugged her hard again. "How long can you stay?"

Katie didn't want to, but she moved away from him. "Well, I don't know how you're going to feel about this, but I'm moving here."

"What?"

She turned to see his confused expression.

Oh, hell. She'd made a horrible mistake. All the happiness she'd been feeling left her.

"Don't worry. I don't mean here to your apartment. I mean London." She cleared her throat, as that last word had come out a little squeaky. He probably didn't want her so close all the time, and she couldn't blame him for being shocked. She still wasn't used to the idea herself.

"Why?" he asked, carefully moving closer to her.

"Well." She bit her lip. "Mar needed someone to open a European branch of the agency and I volunteered." That was close enough to the truth. How could she tell

him she'd arranged everything so she could be with
him? But he'd been coming to see her, so that had to
mean something.

"I'm staying at the Dorchester until I can find a place
to live and a proper office for the agency. I'm hoping to
have everything up and running by the New Year."

There was a full thirty seconds of silence and Katie's
despair only grew.

"The gang at the office thinks it's a good idea to
have someone closer to our European clients. I wanted
to make a change, so here I am."

If he didn't say something soon, she'd have to leave.
Tears already threatened and she refused to let him see
her lose it. She knew he cared about her, but—

"Is that the only reason? The business?" This time
he crossed the floor and took her in his arms again.

"What do you mean?"

"Did you only come to London to start a new job?"

She shrugged. "Are you asking me if I agreed to come
here because of you?"

"That's exactly what I'm asking," he said, his tone
serious.

Katie couldn't look him in the eyes, but she had to
tell the truth. Once she put her heart out there, he would
know everything and she would be exposed. It wasn't a
place she liked to be.

"Yes."

His mouth captured hers before she could finish the
word.

"So I'm guessing it's okay?" she said against his
lips.

"Katie, it's more than okay. I love you. I couldn't
stand being away from you for one more day. I was

ready to chuck everything to be with you. I was going to come up with a plan where I told the dean to let me move to the States and continue my research there, or I was done."

Katie stroked his chin. "Crazy man. You can't do that. There are people depending on you here."

"I don't care. There is only one person who matters to me anymore, and she's in my arms. I would do anything to keep her there."

A tear rolled down Katie's cheek. She couldn't stop the damn thing. Why did that always happen around this man?

"I know you don't like to cry, so I'll just get rid of this for you." He thumbed the tear away. "Now tell me what's wrong?"

Her throat was full of emotion. "You love me?"

"Yes, I do. I love you more than anything. I should have told you before you left, but I wanted to be sure. I've discovered this love thing is like a virulent bacteria—it only grows wilder and stronger as the days pass."

"Bacteria." Katie giggled. "You're so romantic." Her dotty old professor loved her. Katie's world brightened with the realization.

"I love you, too." She gave a happy sigh. "More than anything. I didn't think twice about leaving everything behind. I wanted to be with you so much it hurt."

Mac took her hand in his. "Come on. We need to go."

Surprised, she stumbled after him. "Where are we going?"

"To get your things from the Dorchester. Once I have

you in my bed this time, Katie, you'll never want to leave again."

And she knew he was right.

Epilogue

Seven months later

"Is my tie straight?" Mac asked Katie. She turned to check it for him.

The woman, his woman, was resplendent in a frothy cornflower-blue dress that fit her body perfectly. She looked good enough to eat and he wasn't sure he should let her go out in public. She was nothing short of a wild distraction.

After fiddling with his tie, she touched his cheek. "You're so handsome."

Mac wrapped his arms lightly around her, careful to keep from wrinkling her dress. "And you are a gorgeous creature who is sure to upstage the bride today." He kissed her gently.

She gave him a sweet smile. "Trust me, when you see Mar in her wedding dress you'll change your mind. She's the most beautiful woman I've ever seen, and I swear she's almost glowing with happiness." She glanced at the bedside clock in their hotel suite. "I need to get back to

Mar's room—it's almost time. I just wanted to tell you I loved you."

"Love you, too," he said as he followed her out the door. He had to be down the hallway where the other groomsmen were waiting. He'd been honored when Jackson asked him to join the wedding party. The men had become great friends several months ago when he was helping Katie with one of her cases.

Mar had joined him the last two weeks of his stay, and in between their work they'd all spent a great deal of time together. Mac smiled as he entered the room where all the groomsmen had gathered. There were cigars and whiskey being passed around.

Yes, he'd fit in with her friends, and his friends thought she was just as amazing as he did. Their lives had blended quite easily.

He worried Katie had sacrificed too much and she'd eventually regret her decision, but it had been seven months, and, if anything, she was happier than she'd ever been. That made him happier than any man had a right to be.

He noticed Jackson wasn't smoking or drinking.

Mac patted Jackson's shoulder. "You doing okay? Nerves?"

Jackson smiled. "Nah, man. I'm just ready to marry the woman of my dreams."

"All right, then, let's do this thing," Mac told him as he guided him out the door.

KATIE AND MAC STOOD in a large circle of guests as they watched the happy couple during their first dance. The moment made tears brim.

"Your eyes are about to leak again," Mac warned,

handing her a tissue. He'd kept a steady supply for her throughout the day.

She cleared her throat. "Allergies. I told you that."

"Uh-huh." He winked at her.

Mac knew her too well.

"They're so happy. And you know the best part?"

"What's that?" He took her in his arms.

"We have that, Mac. I didn't think I'd ever find it, but I have it with you."

Mac kissed her long and hard. He didn't care what the other guests might think.

They parted and he lifted her left hand. "So has all this corny wedding stuff changed your mind? Can we finally set a date?"

The man never gave up. "You and my mother. I swear the two of you are conspiring together." That wasn't far from the truth. Her family had loved Mac as soon as they'd met him. They loved him even more when they heard he'd proposed to her.

Her mind drifted to that moment. He'd taken her to the greenhouse with her rosebush, and proposed to her there. It had been so meaningful. Her eyes had leaked profusely that day, too.

"Hey, we don't have to talk about it tonight, hon. You know I'm just having some fun with you."

She smiled at him and glanced at the ring on her hand. The sapphire was surrounded by two rows of diamonds. He'd picked a ring that suited her perfectly. "I'll marry you tomorrow if you want."

Confusion swarmed Mac's face. "Really? That's not just the wedding talking?"

She wrapped her arms around his neck. "I'm serious,

Mac. I'm ready. I've been ready, but you know me. I don't like being pushed into things."

Mac closed his eyes and squeezed her tightly. "My Katie."

She loved it when he called her that.

"I want a winter wedding," she said. "Simple, at my family's church in the Bronx. Maybe we could even do it over Christmas break?"

Mac let out a whoop and twirled her around. The people around them laughed.

"So I guess that's okay with you?"

He kissed her. "Yes. It's your day, Katie. We'll do it any way you want. As long as you become my wife, I don't care about anything else."

His wife. Those words sounded lovely to her.

And Mac would be her husband. Those words were even lovelier. He'd taught her how to love, and she owed him so much. She couldn't imagine her life without him.

"There's just one thing, though," she murmured close to his lips.

He pulled back and eyed her cautiously. "What's that?"

"You have to call my mom and tell her."

Mac started laughing, and before long she had to pat his back.

"It's not funny. I'm her only daughter and the woman loves weddings. You're going to have to keep her in check."

Mac caught his breath. "I think between your father, grandfather and me we can keep her in check. If that's your only concern, I can handle it."

Katie wasn't sure he had any idea what he was in for, but she smiled at him.

Mac kissed her again. "I love you, Katie McClure."

She sighed happily in his arms.

"I love you, too, Professor Douglas."

He took her hand and led her to the dance floor, for what would be the first in a lifetime of dances.

* * * * *

COMING NEXT MONTH

Available April 26, 2011

#609 DELICIOUS DO-OVER
Spring Break
Debbi Rawlins

#610 HIGH STAKES SEDUCTION
Uniformly Hot!
Lori Wilde

#611 JUST SURRENDER...
Harts of Texas
Kathleen O'Reilly

#612 JUST FOR THE NIGHT
24 Hours: Blackout
Tawny Weber

#613 TRUTH AND DARE
Candace Havens

#614 BREATHLESS DESCENT
Texas Hotzone
Lisa Renee Jones

You can find more information on upcoming
Harlequin® titles, free excerpts and more at
www.HarlequinInsideRomance.com.

REQUEST YOUR FREE BOOKS!
2 FREE NOVELS PLUS 2 FREE GIFTS!

❧ Harlequin®

Blaze™

red-hot reads!

YES! Please send me 2 FREE Harlequin® Blaze® novels and my 2 FREE gifts (gifts are worth about $10). After receiving them, if I don't wish to receive any more books, I can return the shipping statement marked "cancel." If I don't cancel, I will receive 6 brand-new novels every month and be billed just $4.24 per book in the U.S. or $4.71 per book in Canada. That's a saving of at least 15% off the cover price. It's quite a bargain. Shipping and handling is just 50¢ per book in the U.S. and 75¢ per book in Canada.* I understand that accepting the 2 free books and gifts places me under no obligation to buy anything. I can always return a shipment and cancel at any time. Even if I never buy another book, the two free books and gifts are mine to keep forever.

151/351 HDN FC4T

Name _____ (PLEASE PRINT) _____

Address _____ Apt. #

City _____ State/Prov. _____ Zip/Postal Code

Signature (if under 18, a parent or guardian must sign)

Mail to the **Reader Service:**
IN U.S.A.: P.O. Box 1867, Buffalo, NY 14240-1867
IN CANADA: P.O. Box 609, Fort Erie, Ontario L2A 5X3

Not valid for current subscribers to Harlequin Blaze books.

Want to try two free books from another line?
Call 1-800-873-8635 or visit www.ReaderService.com.

* Terms and prices subject to change without notice. Prices do not include applicable taxes. Sales tax applicable in N.Y. Canadian residents will be charged applicable taxes. Offer not valid in Quebec. This offer is limited to one order per household. All orders subject to credit approval. Credit or debit balances in a customer's account(s) may be offset by any other outstanding balance owed by or to the customer. Please allow 4 to 6 weeks for delivery. Offer available while quantities last.

Your Privacy—The Reader Service is committed to protecting your privacy. Our Privacy Policy is available online at www.ReaderService.com or upon request from the Reader Service.

We make a portion of our mailing list available to reputable third parties that offer products we believe may interest you. If you prefer that we not exchange your name with third parties, or if you wish to clarify or modify your communication preferences, please visit us at www.ReaderService.com/consumerchoice or write to us at Reader Service Preference Service, P.O. Box 9062, Buffalo, NY 14269. Include your complete name and address.

HB11

*With an evil force hell-bent on destruction,
two enemies must unite to find a truth that turns
all-too-personal when passions collide.*

*Enjoy a sneak peek in Jenna Kernan's next installment
in her original TRACKER series, GHOST STALKER,
available in May, only from Harlequin Nocturne.*

"**W**ho are you?" he snarled.

Jessie lifted her chin. "Your better."

His smile was cold. "Such arrogance could only come from a Niyanoka."

She nodded. "Why are you here?"

"I don't know." He glanced about her room. "I asked the birds to take me to a healer."

"And they have done so. Is that *all* you asked?"

"No. To lead them away from my friends." His eyes fluttered and she saw them roll over white.

Jessie straightened, preparing to flee, but he roused himself and mastered the momentary weakness. His eyes snapped open, locking on her.

Her heart hammered as she inched back.

"Lead who away?" she whispered, suddenly afraid of the answer.

"The ghosts. Nagi sent them to attack me so I would bring them to her."

The wolf must be deranged because Nagi did not send ghosts to attack living creatures. He captured the evil ones after their death if they refused to walk the Way of Souls, forcing them to face judgment.

"Her? The healer you seek is also female?"

"Michaela. She's Niyanoka, like you. The last Seer of Souls and Nagi wants her dead."

HNEXP0511

Jessie fell back to her seat on the carpet as the possibility of this ricocheted in her brain. Could it be true?

"Why should I believe you?" But she knew why. His black aura, the part that said he had been touched by death. Only a ghost could do that. But it made no sense.

Why would Nagi hunt one of her people and why would a Skinwalker want to protect her? She had been trained from birth to hate the Skinwalkers, to consider them a threat.

His intent blue eyes pinned her. Jessie felt her mouth go dry as she considered the impossible. Could the trickster be speaking the truth? Great Mystery, what evil was this?

She stared in astonishment. There was only one way to find her answers. But she had never even met a Skinwalker before and so did not even know if they dreamed.

But if he dreamed, she would have her chance to learn the truth.

Look for GHOST STALKER by Jenna Kernan, available May only from Harlequin Nocturne, wherever books and ebooks are sold.